BELIEVING THE HERO

HEROES OF FREEDOM RIDGE

TARA GRACE ERICSON

Believing the Hero
Heroes of Freedom Ridge Book 9
Copyright © 2021 Tara Grace Ericson and Silver Fountain Press
All Rights Reserved

No part of this book may be used or reproduced in any manner whatsoever without written permission, except in the case of brief quotations embedded in critical articles and reviews. The unauthorized reproduction or distribution of this copyrighted work is illegal. No part of this book may be scanned, uploaded or distributed via the Internet or any other means, electronic or print, without the author's permission.

This book is a work of fiction. The names, characters, places, and incidents are products of the writer's imagination or have been used fictitiously and are not to be construed as real. Any resemblance to persons, living or dead, actual events, locale or organizations is entirely coincidental. The author does not have any control over and does not assume any responsibility for third-party websites or their content.

Holy Bible, New International Version®, NIV® Copyright ©1973, 1978, 1984, 2011 by Biblica, Inc.® Used by permission. All rights reserved worldwide.

Published in the United States of America
Cover Designer: Amanda Walker PA & Design Services
Editor: Editing Done Write
Ebook ISBN: 978-1-949896-22-0
Paperback ISBN: 978-1-949896-23-7

To Little C.
Keep working hard.

For God gave us a spirit not of fear but of power and love and self-control.

— 2 Timothy 1:7

CONTENTS

Chapter 1	1
Chapter 2	14
Chapter 3	25
Chapter 4	37
Chapter 5	43
Chapter 6	49
Chapter 7	61
Chapter 8	71
Chapter 9	81
Chapter 10	91
Chapter 11	99
Chapter 12	104
Chapter 13	117
Chapter 14	127
Chapter 15	132
Chapter 16	139
Chapter 17	144
Chapter 18	153
Chapter 19	164
Chapter 20	174
Epilogue	185
Jan's Pumpkin Snickerdoodles	191
Book 10 of the Heroes of Freedom Ridge	193
Other Books in the Heroes of Freedom Ridge Series	195
Other Books by Tara Grace Ericson	197
Books by Tara Grace Ericson	199
About the Author	201
Acknowledgments	203

1

Jan Clark quickly grabbed a lemon blueberry scone from the bakery case and set it on a plate before sliding it across the narrow counter to the waiting customer.

"Your drink will be right up, Addison. Tell Ty to come see me and to bring Partner with him. I've got a pup cup of whipped cream with his name on it." Addison and Ty had rescued the cutest dog last year, and it had been the start of a relationship for the hotel clerk and one of Freedom Ridge's finest officers. Jan flashed a smile before turning to the next customer in line. "Oh, Derek! How are you? How is Megan?" Jan asked, referring to Derek's wife. They'd gotten married just over a year ago after being stranded together in a blizzard.

"Hey, Mrs. Clark. I'm good. Megan is good, but

she's dreading these colder days as they roll in. I think that Alabama blood must freeze at about fifty degrees."

Jan chuckled. "She did come in here with a scarf the other day. Pretty sure the man in front of her was still wearing shorts."

Derek laughed. "Sounds about right."

"Are you staying here today or do you need your drink to go?"

"I'm actually meeting up with Aiden."

Jan couldn't help but smile at the mention of her only son. Though he was creeping towards his mid-thirties, Aiden was her pride and joy. Well, with the possible exception of the grandchild he'd gifted her last summer. Being a grandmother felt like the calling her life had been missing for years.

As though summoned by the mention of his name, her son strolled through the door of Stories and Scones with a wide smile.

"Hey, Mom."

"Hey, sweetie. Shouldn't you be sleeping?" If her memory served her correctly—though it was less reliable with each passing year—Aiden's shift at the fire station would start later today.

He shrugged in response. "Probably, but Landon woke everyone in the neighborhood up this morning bright and early. Plus, Derek and I were due to catch up."

While her son and his friend grabbed their drinks and found a table, Jan switched back into manager mode. A quick glance confirmed that her staff was handling the drink prep and drive-thru orders. For once, they didn't need anything from her. Managing the combination bookstore and coffee shop had once seemed like a foolish dream. The kind of business everyone wants to own or visit but that never actually succeeds.

Here in Freedom, it was a different story. When she opened Stories and Scones a few years after her husband died, the store had been welcomed with open arms. Now, she did a brisk business of locals and tourists combined. The tourists loved her selection of Colorado authors, and the coffee kept the locals coming regularly. She was never bored while the store was open.

Stories and Scones had been a welcome distraction after James died. Aiden was away at college at that point, and Jan traded her quiet days as an online teacher for the constant movement of the bakery.

The bells on the door jingled and she glanced up from the carafe of cold brew she was prepping for the following day.

Petey.

Jan smoothed her short hair back behind her ear.

Pete O'Rourke stopped by the shop nearly every day. Just another regular. Except that wasn't true. Jan had known him since high school, and when he had returned to Freedom after retiring from some federal government desk job, they'd quickly become friends again.

"Good morning, Petey." She fought a smirk at the nickname she knew he disliked.

Pete rolled his eyes. "It makes me feel like I'm ten years old on the playground when you call me that, you know."

Jan chuckled. "You know what they say: age is just a number."

"Ha, well some days my number feels about twenty higher than it should."

She knew how he felt. Despite being in her late fifties, there were times Jan felt much older. Losing your life partner would do that. So would the aches and pains of someone who went skiing nearly every season and had the injuries to prove it.

"Your usual?"

"Yep. And throw in a box with half a dozen scones for me. I've got someone checking into a cabin this morning and want to welcome them."

Jan raised her eyebrow as she packaged the scones. "That's new. Are these folks special? Or will you be welcoming all your renters like this? I can cut you a deal on bulk scone orders," she added with a wink.

Pete shook his head. "Nice try. Don't mix up that

extra dough quite yet. These ones are special. I guess the mother has cancer, and this is likely to be their last trip as a family. Just trying to help make it memorable."

Jan felt the tug of emotion at the thought of a family left without their mother. "Is she young?" The teasing in her voice was gone now.

Pete pressed his lips together with a slight nod. "Yeah. Kids are still at home. Three of them."

Her exhalation held a slight hum of empathy. That was terrible.

She handed him the scones and began to package some cookies. "I'll be praying for them."

"Me too." And Jan knew enough about Pete to know he meant it.

Pete stepped back toward the register, but Jan waved a hand. "On the house." She handed him the bag of cookies. "These too."

He gave a sad smile, his gray eyes meeting hers. "Thanks. I'll be sure to tell them so they know where to get more." Then he widened the smile and winked at her. "After all, your sugar cookies are addictive."

Jan felt the blush in her cheeks and resisted the urge to cool the heat with her hand. Before she could linger too much on why a simple compliment from a friend made her red, the young woman working the drive-thru called her name and signaled her over.

"That's my cue," she said.

"I'll see you tomorrow night for cards, right?" Pete asked.

She nodded. The monthly night of playing cards with Art and Issy Pembroke was always a good time. Pete waved as he pushed the door open by walking backwards through it.

An hour later, Aiden stopped by the counter again.

"I'm headed out, Mom. Do you need anything?"

"I need to see that grandbaby of mine. Aren't you and Joanna due for a night out? You can bring Landon to my place and have an evening alone." Jan never said no to a chance to see her grandson, but she knew Aiden and Joanna were hesitant to ask her too often. Even now, she could see the inclination to decline her offer on his face.

"I insist," she quickly interjected. She would gladly enjoy an evening stacking blocks and chasing Landon around the house. The alternative was another night spent watching crime documentaries and ignoring the emptiness that seemed to haunt the house she had once shared with her husband.

"Are you sure? We don't want to put you out."

Jan shot him a look. "That's ridiculous, Aiden. What exactly would you be pulling me away from? It's not as though I have an overflowing social calendar." She tried to keep the bitterness from coloring her tone, though she wasn't entirely sure she was successful. Jan wasn't unhappy. She had a wonderful life filled with faithful friends, a beautiful family, a rewarding career, and the reassurance of a solid faith in Christ. Still, evenings spent alone were long.

"I'll talk to Jo. Maybe this weekend will work. After tomorrow, my next shift starts Monday."

"Let me know. I'm happy to help." She came around the counter and wrapped her arms around Aiden. He was six inches taller than her and had the same strong build as his father, who had also been a firefighter. She squeezed Aiden's waist before stepping back. Her most fervent prayer each day was that God would protect her son.

"Be safe at work, sweetie."

BACK IN HIS OFFICE, three doors down from Stories and Scones, Pete readied the paperwork for the reservation coming in today. In addition to his insurance agency, Pete owned half a dozen cabins in the mountains for short-term rentals. From honeymooners to families looking to hike to reclusive authors looking for an escape—Pete had hosted them all.

Of course, then there was the family checking in today. A terminal diagnosis and just enough time to enjoy one last family getaway.

Pete sighed. He had already heavily discounted the reservation, claiming an off-season special when Mr. Kizner had asked why it was lower than advertised. But he wanted to do more. They would be here for three weeks, so he still had some time to figure out exactly how to pull that off.

Pete punched the code into the small safe tucked behind a painting in his office. On the inside wall hung eight sets of keys, carefully color-coded and labeled with cabin numbers.

His eyes fell on the unlabeled key with a black cap on it. That cabin wasn't one he rented out, but he did need to take a trip up the mountain and make sure it was in good shape.

It was probably unorthodox for a small-town insurance agent to have what amounted to a safe house. It was, however, almost cliche for a retired CIA operations officer.

Overdone as it might be, Pete couldn't shake the need for a place with no paper trail, flawless defensive positioning, and a stash of rations and weapons that could last him for months if needed. He'd spent too many years on foreign soil, often vulnerable except for his own careful steps to be prepared for any possibility.

And prepared he would be, even in quiet Freedom, Colorado. Of course, despite the sleepy reputation of the tourist town, Pete's safe house had actually served its purpose last year when his friend Heath needed a hideout to protect someone. He owned a security firm in Freedom Ridge called Got Your Six.

Heath had recognized the operative in Pete from the moment they met. His own experience in military intelligence meant they shared a special bond. He and Jeremiah were the only people in Freedom who knew the truth about Pete's "boring" government job. As far as anyone else knew, Pete had lived in Virginia and worked for the Geological Survey. Nobody stayed overly interested when you told them you monitored river and stream levels.

The truth was far more interesting. And far more haunting.

"Hello?" The voice came from the front room of the office. Most likely his guests, or an insurance client.

Pete called back, "I'll be right with you." His assistant, Heath's sister Tessa, had the day off.

He grabbed the keys with the red tag for cabin four. Then he shut the safe firmly, wishing he could just as easily close the door on the memories he carried.

Jan arranged her cards by suit and number in her hand, carefully positioning them so Pete couldn't sneak a glance while he grabbed a drink, like he was known to do. She smiled when she moved the queen of spades. It was easier to avoid those points if she could choose when to play it.

Card night with the Pembrokes was a long-standing tradition. What had started as a gathering with a few couples from their small group had grown to a rotating group of about a dozen individuals. A handful of married couples jumped in and out, along with Jan and Pete and a few older singles.

Art and Isabella Pembroke owned the Freedom Ridge Fudge Factory, which sat between her shop and Pete's office on Main Street, along with Wick and Sarcasm. Ashley, the owner of the candle shop, sometimes joined them for cards as well.

The game varied depending on who came and how the numbers landed. Tonight, it was just the four of them. Pete grabbed a cookie from the container she'd brought, then sat down. He held the cookie in his mouth while he picked up his cards. She smiled at the ridiculous sight of the jumbo cooking hanging out of his mouth. He finally took a bite and set the rest on the table while moving his cards.

"These are delicious, Jan. New recipe?"

She nodded. "Trying it out for fall in the shop. It's a pumpkin snickerdoodle."

From across the table, Art mumbled his approval through a full mouth. After he swallowed, he echoed Pete's thoughts. "Seriously, these are awesome. Nutmeg?"

"I know it's controversial, but I think it gives them that autumn feel."

"As long as you don't put it in apple pie, I'm a big fan," Isabella said with a laugh.

Art rolled his eyes with a smile. "Not this again."

Jan chuckled. The Pembrokes had been disagreeing about the merits of nutmeg in apple pie for decades.

Pete chimed in. "One of these days, we just need to have a taste test and settle the debate once and for all."

"Oh, that sounds fun," Issy said.

"Maybe in November during card night we can make it happen," Jan said. "I can make both versions, and I promise not to tell which is which."

Art smiled. "Fine. You'll all see how right I am when you taste it. For now, can we just play cards? I'm ready to beat Pete for once."

Pete laughed. "You can try, Art."

The game started when Pete threw out the two of clubs. Jan desperately tried to control her grin when she managed to sneak the queen of spades into a trick that Pete had won.

When all the cards had been played, Pete was gloating good-naturedly about his victory until Jan cleared her throat. When he looked up at her, she pointed silently at the pile of face-up cards in front of him.

He looked down. "What?"

She pointed again. He narrowed his eyes and searched through the stack until he saw the queen. His mouth dropped open. "When did that happen?"

Laughter broke out around the table at his dumbfounded expression. Jan covered her mouth, shaking with laughter. Pete was a good sport, though he pretended to pout.

"I suppose I deserved that," he joked.

Jan grinned. Fellowship with these people did her heart good.

There was a knock on the door and the Pembroke's daughter poked her head in. She waved as she ran past. "Don't mind me! Darren forgot his Spiderman figure and, obviously, it's a catastrophe!"

Moments later, she ran back out. "Bye, Mom. Bye, Dad. See you tomorrow."

Jan grinned. Darren was a sweet six-year-old boy who Sabrina was raising on her own.

Issy shook her head. "Darren sleeps with that

Spiderman every night. Does Landon have anything like that yet?"

She nodded. "Oh yeah. He is pretty attached to his llama lovey."

Art smiled. "I remember when Sabrina was little, she had a stuffed pony that went absolutely everywhere with her. It got lost somewhere along a road trip, probably left behind in a hotel room or something. Anyway, you would have thought the world ended! Issy ended up buying her a new one and telling her we'd miraculously found it in our suitcase."

Jan laughed. "Aiden's was a Transformer robot. My sister gave it to him, and I think that toy used a set of batteries every other week. It was so loud. At one point, James told him they didn't make batteries for it anymore."

Although he listened and laughed, his smiles didn't quite reach his gray eyes. Pete was awfully quiet as they traded funny stories about their kids and grandkids.

She turned to him. "Pete, what was your favorite toy as a kid?"

After he'd answered and Art had begun to answer the same question, he gave her a grateful smile that warmed her soul, his silver eyes once again filled with light.

2

Sunday morning, Jan tucked her Bible and purse along the back counter of the coffee station in the church lobby.

A sharply dressed young man greeted her. Kyle Prince was the Connections and Young Adults Pastor at Freedom Bible Church. "I really appreciate you volunteering for this. You wouldn't believe how hard it is to find people willing to serve."

Jan looked around at the coffee bar stocked with mini-muffins, donut holes, and coffeemakers. "Happy to help. Just tell me what to do!" She'd filled her coffee cup from the other side of the counter for years but hadn't volunteered before. It had always seemed a bit too on-the-nose for the coffee shop owner to be volunteering at the church coffee bar.

"We'll just wait a minute and see if your covolunteer arrives."

"Oh? Who's my partner in crime?"

"I guess that would be me."

Jan's face broke into a smile as she turned toward the familiar voice. Pete stepped around the corner of the counter with a shrug.

"Hey now! Nobody warned me I had to work with him." She let laughter color her tone as she winked at Pastor Kyle.

He gave her an apologetic smile, his eyes full of amusement. "Sorry, no exchanges."

Pete faked pulling a knife from his chest with a wounded look. He was a good sport. "Good morning to you, too, Kyle."

"Good to see you, Pete. I was telling Jan how hard it was to get volunteers to run the coffee bar, so I really appreciate both of you signing up."

"I can't imagine it will be so terrible. Make some coffee, refill the pastries, and greet people as they caffeinate. What's so hard about that?" Pete looked at her for an answer.

"Beats me. We'll show them how it's done."

Kyle grinned. "Well, all right. Let me show you how the equipment works and where to find everything you'll need." The young pastor was animated, talking quickly as he gave them the tour.

He walked them through the coffee bar, pointing out the spare cups and lids under the cabinets. "We don't have room for all the extra creamers in here, so you'll have to get them from the main kitchen. They are above the fridge."

Jan nodded. He quickly showed them how to make the large pots of coffee, his high-energy nature grating slightly on Jan's uncaffeinated nerves. By the time they placed the newly filled thermos on the counter, people were starting to trickle in for the early service. Someone called Kyle's name across the lobby and waved for him to come over. He held up a finger and turned back to them.

"I think that's all. You guys just need to stay out here until ten minutes after service starts, and cover the pastry trays behind the counter before you go in. There is another crew covering the time between services."

"Sounds good," Pete responded.

"We've got this, Pastor. Go ahead and go."

He flashed a grateful smile. "Thanks. I'll check back with you before I head into service."

Jan took a deep breath and turned to Pete, who was only inches away. "He's kind of exhausting, isn't he?"

Pete chuckled, and the low, warm sound had Jan's nerves on high alert. The space inside the small coffee station seemed even tighter, despite having one less person than a minute ago. "He's definitely enthusiastic.

Jan took a step back, busying herself arranging muffins on a serving tray. "How has your weekend been? How is that family you checked in?" It seemed important to find a safe topic of conversation. It always did with Pete. She was often tempted to share too much with her longtime friend, especially when he studied her with his dark-gray eyes. Sometimes, it felt like he could see her every thought. She was probably reading too much into it. Pete was a handsome man, but he was just a friend.

"My weekend is good so far. I'm hoping to take a hike this afternoon while the weather is still good. The family is all checked in. I invited them to church, so maybe we will see them today."

"That was a good idea," Jan said. "I hope they take you up on it."

"Me too." Pete looked around the coffee bar. "You're the boss. What do we need to do?"

"Why am I the boss?"

Pete raised an eyebrow. "You think I should be in charge?"

Jan coughed a laugh. "Okay, you might be right. We probably need to get these pastries out front. Can you grab the tray while I grab napkins?" They stocked the table and made another pot of coffee. A steady stream of churchgoers filtered through the lobby, chatting in small groups as children zigzagged around the standing-height tables.

While Pete talked to a friend, Jan noted the pastry table was running low. She brought out another container of muffins and arranged them on the table, laughing when Haven Gilbert's daughter, Miah, snuck up to the table. The seven-year-old put one finger to her mouth and gave Jan the universal signal for quiet. She snagged two donut holes before scampering off again.

"Gigi!"

Jan turned to see Landon toddling toward her, Joanna and Aiden trailing behind with amused smiles. She scooped up her grandson and smothered him in kisses. "Good morning, big boy!" He looked adorable in a button-down shirt that matched Aiden's. "I can't believe Aiden lets you dress them in matching clothes, Joanna. James would never go for it, even for family pictures!"

Joanna held up her hands. "Don't look at me. Aiden got Landon dressed this morning."

Aiden gave a guilty smile. "He's just so cute."

Jan laughed at her son's admission. In her arms, Landon was straining toward the table of baked goods. "You want one? Don't tell Mama I spoiled you." Jan winked at her daughter-in-law and tipped the eager toddler down so he could grab a muffin. He held it up triumphantly with a toothy grin. Jan unwrapped the muffin and handed it back to him.

She felt Pete step into their small circle. "Oh

wow! Is that for me, Landon? Thank you!" He opened his hand, asking for the muffin. Laughter rang out when Landon stuffed the whole muffin in his mouth instead.

On the other side of the wall, the music started in the sanctuary. Jan passed Landon back to his parents so they could head into service. The little boy waved happily at Pete as they walked away. Jan watched as Pete made silly faces at her grandson, sending him into a fit of happy giggles. Pete would have made a great father. Out of respect for his privacy, she'd never asked why he never had a family, but it didn't stop her curiosity.

He wasn't even sixty. Technically, he could find himself a young wife and still have one. He was in better physical shape than most of the men who walked into her shop each day, regardless of their age. His face wore the markers of time gracefully. She wouldn't consider herself vain, but she wasn't oblivious to how her once shiny brown hair had dulled and started to thin.

Pete's dark hair was sprinkled with salt, especially around his temples. Her fingers twitched with the urge to brush it there. His face turned toward her and Jan jerked, trying to disguise the fact that she'd basically been ogling him.

"Should we start cleaning things up?"

Her throat still tight from the threat of embarrassment, Jan nodded in response. This was ridiculous. She was a grown woman, daydreaming like a high schooler with a crush. Even as she watched Pete interact with her grandson, she couldn't help but think of how her husband, James, would have done the same.

What would he have looked like as his hairline continued to recede and his mustache turned gray?

But James wasn't here anymore. So why did it feel so much like betraying him to let her thoughts dwell on Pete's admirable qualities?

PETE CLEARED the table as Jan restocked the coffee corner with cups, napkins, and stirring sticks. The spread wasn't as fancy as some of the larger churches in Denver that basically had the same equipment in their lobby as Jan had inside Stories and Scones.

She got his attention quietly and said, "I'm going to find the extra creamers in the kitchen."

Pete nodded in acknowledgement and she walked away.

When Jan hadn't returned a minute later, Pete made his way to the church kitchen to see if she needed help. Once inside the door, he was greeted with the unsettling sight of Jan on a small stool, reaching awkwardly for the large box of individual-sized coffee creamers in the cabinet above the fridge.

"Jan, are you crazy? If you fall, Aiden will never forgive me."

"I got it," she insisted, straining a little farther and pushing onto her tiptoes.

"Oh, for crying out loud," Pete muttered, stepping next to her.

She stepped backwards with a small stumble, and his breath caught. His hands found her waist to steady her.

She stepped down carefully, but his hands stayed on her hips, just in case. What was she thinking? They weren't in their thirties. He knew Jan was active and capable, but if he walked in to find her sprawled on the floor at the bottom of the ladder, he was going to have a heart attack. And then they'd both be in trouble.

Her bright eyes twinkled with laughter. "See? I told you I had it."

Pete just shook his head. She was safely on the ground and so close he could see the flecks of gold in her eyes—eyes that would be far too easy to lose himself in. He stepped back, releasing his grip, and checked his watch. He cleared his throat, then asked, "Is that all we need?"

Back at the coffee corner, they finished stocking the creamer and wiping down the tables. Just a minute before they were supposed to go into service, a family of five stepped cautiously into the lobby.

Pete immediately recognized the family from the cabin rental. "Hey, good morning. How are the Kizners today?"

"Hey, Pete. Are we too late?"

Pete shook his head. "No, not at all. They're still on the second song." He glanced around and waved Jan over. "Are we all done out here? I'd like to walk the Kizners inside. Mike, Shelly, this is Jan. She made the delicious scones in your welcome box."

"Nice to meet you, Jan. Pete's a lucky guy to be married to such a great baker." Mike Kizner's words had heat rising up the collar of Pete's shirt.

"Oh, we're not together. Just friends. It's so nice to meet you all." Jan's correction was kind, but her amusement was obvious.

Pete resisted the urge to frown. Why was the idea of them together funny to her?

She continued, "I think we're all done, though. Let's all head in and find a seat together."

Jan had a gift for making people feel at ease, and he caught the small smile Shelly sent her. Jan probably would have made a good asset. The evaluation came unbidden and was dismissed just as easily. The idea of honest, reliable Jan willingly deceiving anyone was a ludicrous thought. Even more important was the fact that he needed to stop seeing the world through the lens of an agent. People didn't really fall into neat categories—asset or liability—like they did for an operative.

He followed the family into the sanctuary and to the seats Jan was guiding them into. She stood at the end of the row with her arm out, gesturing for him to go in ahead of her.

Instead, he leaned close to her. "Ladies first," he whispered when he was close enough to be heard over the sounds of the worship song. Her scent flooded his senses, the aroma of her floral perfume mixing with that of rising bread dough.

He stepped back, allowing her into the row of chairs, and followed her in. In the dark of the worship center, Pete's awareness went on hyperdrive. He could feel Jan next to him, and the urge to hold her hand was nearly overwhelming. He'd always thought she was beautiful. Vivacious and kind, Jan brightened his days with her presence. Losing her husband couldn't have been easy, but was there any possibility that she would be interested in something more with him?

The song ended and they took their seats. He struggled to keep his mind on the sermon instead of stealing glances at Jan. During one such glance, she turned to him and gave him a look she'd likely perfected giving to Aiden while he misbehaved in church. Apparently, Pete's stolen looks weren't very sneaky. So much for his spy craft.

After service, he and Jan said goodbye to the Kizner family. Before she could dart off, Pete touched her arm. "I've got a dinner event to go to in Denver next Friday for the insurance board. Would you want to keep me company? It promises to be about as exciting as a teeth cleaning, but the food will be good."

Didn't that sound appealing? Who wouldn't want to come with that ringing endorsement?

Jan's smile fell. "Oh, I'm sorry, Pete. I can't on Friday. I promised to babysit for Aiden and Jo. I'm sure it won't be as bad as you say, though!"

Pete tucked his disappointment behind a sarcastic smile. Was it just a convenient excuse? "You're probably right. There's nothing I love more than a riveting update on the actuarial tables of Colorado homeowners."

Jan laughed. "See? You'll have a blast."

Someone across the room caught Jan's eye. She waved to them as she said goodbye. "I'll see you tomorrow, Petey?"

With a nod, he confirmed. "Yep, see you tomorrow." He was beginning to wonder if he could stay away from the lovely Jan Clark, even if he tried.

3

By the time 9:30 rolled around each morning, Jan was watching the door for any sign of Pete O'Rourke. She tallied the morning's orders and listened absently to the elderly men of Freedom, gathered at one of the large tables, solving the world's problems over coffee. Pete was as predictable as the sun, and just like clockwork, he stepped through the door at 9:31 on Monday morning.

She'd been replaying their conversation at church since it happened. Had Pete invited her as a friend? Or was it possible that she wasn't the only one who had goosebumps when he'd whispered in her ear in the dim lighting of the worship center?

Truth was, she would have loved to attend his event, despite his lackluster description. It was rare for her to have an occasion to dress up. She couldn't even remember the last time she'd gone into Denver. But she was being honest with Pete when she said she'd agreed to babysit. With Aiden's shift schedule, they rarely ended up with a weekend that worked for date nights. This weekend was for them, and Jan didn't want to ruin it. Even if it meant she missed out on an evening with Pete in a suit. He was always well-dressed, but that meant slacks and button downs. Adding a suit jacket and tie... Was it hot in here?

"Morning, Petey," she greeted him, same as every other day.

Pete held the door for someone out of view, and Jan smiled as Aiden jogged up and into the shop.

"Morning, sweetie."

"Hey, Mom."

"I hear you've got a big date this weekend, Aiden." Confusion filled Aiden's face at Pete's words.

"Well, yeah. But how'd you know?"

Pete's face grew red, and Jan busied herself tallying orders to hide her own blush. "Oh, I, uh, asked your mother to join me for an insurance dinner on Friday, but she turned me down."

Jan stared at the notepad, drawing a blank as to whether she was supposed to be marking a blueberry scone or a blueberry muffin down from the receipt in her hand. Listening to their conversation left no room for other mental tasks, even the most tedious.

Aiden's eagerness was barely disguised. "She can go."

"Aiden, you don't—"

"Oh, no. I didn't mean—"

She and Pete spoke together, then both stopped.

Aiden took advantage of their confusion. "Of course, she'll go. Mom, you should have called me. Jo and I can go another night! Saturday would work just as well for us."

She turned to Pete. Was that hope she saw in his eyes? "Did you already find someone else?"

Pete shook his head. He met and held her gaze before responding, "There's no one else."

Her heart threatened to beat out of her chest and the moment stretched on. Was she hearing more than he intended in those words? He continued to look at her like she was the most important thing on the face of the earth.

"Great!" Aiden's excited voice jerked her from her reverie. "It's a date." He winked at her and then ducked out of the coffee shop. Probably already texting Jo with the news that his mom was going on a date.

"He was so excited, he didn't even stay for his coffee," Pete commented. With his observation, the spell was broken and Jan chuckled. "Look, don't feel like you have to come if you don't want to." Pete looked at the ground with uncharacteristic shyness. "Aiden didn't exactly give you a choice, and I don't want you to feel steamrolled." He hesitated, then met her eyes and continued, "I do hope you'll come, though."

Some rational part of her brain kept stoically insisting he just wanted the company, and that she was just a convenient friend. Another, more hopeful part of her was squealing loudly that there was more to this particular invitation. They'd been friends for years, but lately, something felt different. And the last voice? A quiet whisper of worry that getting involved with anyone was a bad idea.

It had been seven years since James died, though. He was far too young, barely in his fifties. But he'd had a heart attack at the scene of a fire, and her life had changed in an instant. She wasn't sure she could survive going through that again. If Pete was really testing the waters of something more than friendship, was she ready?

Thoughts of the lonely nights and quiet dinners crossed her mind, followed by the easy conversations she'd always shared with Pete.

She held his gaze and smiled. "I'd love to go with you."

Pete's eyes crinkled and his face brightened. "Wonderful. I'll send you the details." She fixed his coffee and said goodbye before he headed back to his office, seemingly excited about the prospect of reviewing every policy up for renewal this month.

Jan chuckled after he left. If they did end up dating, at least she wouldn't have to worry about him running into a burning building or going skydiving like James and Aiden had done. Someone like Pete O'Rourke, with his penchant for paperwork and his habit of misplacing his reading glasses, was about as low risk as she could get.

"Janet," Pete all but breathed her name. "You look… stunning," he finished, feeling like the word was woefully inadequate. Upon hearing that the dinner was black tie, Jan had scolded him for not giving her more notice and then claimed she was calling Joanna. Pete thought he might owe Joanna a thank you note. Or a free night at one of his cabins. The woman standing before him was Jan, but more. Delicate earrings dangled near her neckline, drawing his eyes down to her bare shoulders and exposed collarbone.

A hint of pink tinged her cheeks. "Thank you. You look quite dashing, as well. I can't say I've ever seen you in a tux."

"I'd rather be in my hiking boots," he replied honestly.

Jan clicked her tongue. "It's very James Bond, I have to say. Perhaps we should pretend you are a secret agent tonight."

Pete nearly swallowed his tongue, but Jan was busy wrapping a long shawl around her shoulders.

He cleared his throat. "A secret agent sounds a bit dangerous, don't you think? The insurance board might be opposed to such high-risk behavior."

Jan chuckled at his joke, and he escorted her to his car. The drive to Denver was uneventful, but within the small confines of his car, he could detect every note of her perfume. He offered her control of the radio, pleasantly surprised when she flipped to the classic rock station.

"They don't make music like that anymore," she lamented, as the last notes of "Carry on Wayward Son" were covered by the host's gravelly voice.

"They call it classic for a reason."

"Hmmph. I think that's just code for old."

Pete laughed. "Maybe so."

At the dinner, Pete shook hands with the members he knew. This organization was made up of independent insurance agents from all over central Colorado. The networking had been invaluable when he was opening his own agency, and he liked staying plugged in.

"Jan, I'd like you to meet Michael Shriver. Mike, this is Jan."

"Blink twice if you are being held hostage," Mike stage-whispered to Jan.

Pete wanted to be annoyed at the antics of his friend, but Jan's carefree laughter soothed any hint of irritation. "Nice to meet you, Mike."

"We'll catch up later, Mike. I'm hoping Jan will join me for a dance." Pete held out his hand to her. When her fingers slid into his, Pete felt the touch all the way to his core. Ducking carefully around tables, he led her to the nearly empty dance floor and pulled her into his arms.

How long had it been since he held a woman like this—close enough to see her pulse jump beneath the tender skin of her neck? Close enough to be enveloped in her perfume with every spin and to hear her voice at barely a whisper?

For years, Jan had been a constant in his life. A friend, nothing more. After all, James had still been alive when Pete moved back to Freedom. A few years later, his friend Jan was a widow, grieving the loss of her husband—as Pete grieved the loss of the man who had become a friend as well.

Now, though? Something had shifted and he couldn't pretend his daily visits to Stories and Scones were simply to see a friend and pick up coffee. He had to admit that he came to see the woman who was becoming far more important to him than he ever imagined. It had happened so gradually he wasn't sure he'd be able to pinpoint a single moment that he realized he was falling in love with his closest friend. But slowly and surely, it had.

"Janet," he said softly above the gentle melody of the string quartet, "I'm very glad you were able to join me tonight." It wasn't nearly enough. The words didn't come close to explaining the fervent nature of his joy at being her escort this evening.

Jan's eyes met his and he saw the kindness and goodness there he was accustomed to seeing. "Me too," she replied. "It's been a long time since I've been out with a man."

Her cheeks reddened at her words and she stammered. "Not that this is a real date or anything."

Pete raised his eyebrows. "Isn't it?"

Jan's embarrassed mutterings stopped. "Is it?"

Pete moved his hand from her waist and gently stroked a thumb on her cheek. "I'd very much like it to be. I understand if you're not ready, but I've admired you for years, and I count you among my closest friends. I'd really like to see if there could be more between us…if you're interested."

Jan opened her mouth to respond, then her eyes shifted over his shoulder. He felt the tap on his shoulder and tried not to groan in disappointment. Someone had seriously poor timing, and it wasn't the band. Pete pasted a smile on his face and turned to see Mike holding out a hand.

"Mind if I cut in, Pete? It's hardly fair that you keep the most beautiful woman here tonight all to yourself."

Pete couldn't argue with his assessment of Jan's beauty, but he was definitely irked with his audacity. He stuffed down the possessive urge to send Mike packing and turned to Jan. "I guess that's up to the beautiful lady."

Jan blushed and nodded.

Before he stepped away, he leaned in to whisper, "I'll be waiting to finish that conversation later."

Pete grabbed a drink from the bar and tried not to glare at Mike dancing with Jan as she laughed at something he said. He noticed when someone sidled up next to him but quickly dismissed the observation, until a familiar voice made him freeze mid-swallow.

"White wine, please."

The British accent and smoky voice was one he would recognize anywhere. The question was, why was she here? He forced the liquid down his throat and ignored the need to cough. In five seconds, Pete had surveyed the room, looking for anything out of the ordinary, any threat at all. His eyes went to Jan, still safely in Mike's arms.

"Hello, David. Or should I say, Pete?"

He twisted to meet her stare, silent as he watched her stoically sip her wine.

"Victoria. Or should I say…" He glanced at the name tag on her dress. "Colleen?" He laughed at the absurdity of it.

Her serious facade broke into a smile. "It's good to see you, David. It's been a long time."

"Call me Pete. I was David in a previous life." He'd gone by his middle name as an agent. A modicum of separation from his real life and his life in the field.

"Pete, then."

"Why are you here?"

"Let's dance," she said in lieu of a real answer, setting her full wine glass on the bar and walking toward the dance floor.

Pete sighed and tipped back the last of his drink before following her. When he took her hand, none of the fireworks he'd felt with Jan were present. Interesting. Once, twenty years ago, he'd believed himself in love with Victoria.

"You never did wait for me to agree. Just barging on and assuming I would follow."

"I assume you're referring to Belarus?" Victoria's amusement was evident.

"Sure," he agreed. "And Paris and Istanbul." He crooked a smile. "Going in after you almost got me shot in Berlin."

"Hmm, did I ever thank you for that?"

"If I'm not mistaken, you sent flowers to the hospital."

"We got the intel," she added.

"We saved the girl," he replied. Once upon a time, he might not have been able to say which was more important. But he wasn't the same man anymore.

"Why are you here?" It was the second time he'd asked the question, but there wouldn't be a third. He might respect Victoria. He even liked her on occasion. But right now, she was a threat to everything he'd built in Freedom. No one here knew his past, and no one would. Which meant Victoria needed to disappear back across the Atlantic to whatever embassy she was stationed at.

"There's a threat."

His pulse jumped and he felt himself go on alert. He discreetly glanced around the ballroom again, seeking out an invisible enemy.

"Where?"

"They are looking for you. You need to be careful."

A dozen questions flicked through his mind. "What do they want from me? I'm nobody. Not anymore."

He had made sure of it. Nothing tied him to his past life as an agent. Any intel he might have had once was fifteen years old. In the intelligence community, that might as well be fifty.

The song ended and someone stepped across the stage to the podium. Victoria met his eyes. "Just be careful, Pete. I'll be nearby. You know how to reach me."

"Same protocol?"

Victoria nodded, then slipped away through the crowd. He pushed down the irritation at her exit. She always had a flair for the dramatic. Was that what this was? Or was the other shoe about to drop?

4

Jan bit her lip as Pete watched the beautiful woman walk away from his place on the dance floor. Green wasn't a good color on her, but she couldn't deny the envy she felt at the obvious rapport the woman had with Pete.

Was she just another insurance agent? Or perhaps an old flame? Maybe Jan didn't know Pete as well as she thought.

While they'd been dancing, Jan had heard the British accent, though she hadn't been able to make out the conversation with Mike jabbering in her ear. Jan thought the woman was younger, but her unnaturally smooth skin and muscular arms could have been hiding her true age.

Pete walked toward her with an outstretched

hand, and she laid her own in it, grateful to make that connection again. She was just being insecure. After all, Pete had asked her to this event, not Lucy Longlegs over there. Jan tried to locate the woman in the ballroom but couldn't find her at any of the tables.

"Hey, sorry about that. I hope Mike didn't convince you to switch insurance agents."

A smile tugged at her cheek, since Mike had tried to do exactly that. "He was fine. Who was it you were dancing with?" Desperately trying to sound casual, Jan busied herself adjusting the shawl around her shoulders.

"Just an old friend. Shall we find our seats?"

He dismissed the woman so easily that Jan breathed a bit easier.

Pete pulled out her chair and introduced her to the people he knew at the table. He certainly seemed unaffected by the beautiful Brit. An old friend, he'd said. Jan was certain she had never seen the woman around Freedom before. Was she from Virginia?

Jan refocused on the table around her, making small talk with the husband of another agent and explaining Stories and Scones to another. During the presentations and awards, she was hyperaware of Pete sitting next to her. Their legs brushed a time or two, but he did nothing but watch intently to whatever was happening on stage.

All the buildup from that conversation before and now he was giving her nothing. What was wrong with this man?

Jan crossed her legs and arms, realizing she probably looked a bit like a frustrated toddler. They had the entire ride home from Denver to talk. This was Pete's work event, and he probably just wanted to pay attention. It had nothing to do with the woman whose dress was slit clear up her thigh.

She didn't really even have a right to be jealous anyway. Pete had said he was interested, but they hadn't decided anything. He wasn't *hers*. Oh, but the thought that he might be soon was an enticing thing to consider. Heat had risen all over as he spoke those sweet words to her while they danced.

If she were interested, he had said. Was she?

Jan studied the profile of the human sitting to her right. Strong jaw, piercing eyes, and a kind spirit.

Was she interested?

Yes. Yes, she was.

Pete pulled out of Denver traffic and onto the on ramp for the freeway. What an unwelcome turn the evening had taken.

"Um, Pete?"

He turned toward Jan briefly, then back at the road. "Yeah?"

"Are we going to finish that conversation now?" Jan sounded unsure of herself.

Pete knew instantly what conversation she was referring to. He desperately wanted to finish it, but he also knew that he should be careful. If Victoria was right? If someone from his past was here and looking for him... Starting a relationship with Jan was something he couldn't afford to do.

But what if Victoria was wrong? It had been fifteen years! She had to be mistaken.

He glanced at Jan again, seeing the vulnerability in her eyes. "Absolutely," he replied. "I think I said my part. So, what do you think?"

Jan took a deep breath before speaking. "When James died, a part of me died too. The thought of being with someone else only carried guilt." Pete listened carefully. Hoping. Praying. "It's like I was betraying James with the very consideration."

Pete's heart sank. James was a very lucky man to be loved so completely by this woman. "I understand."

"I don't think you do. I mean, how could you? Unless someone has lost the person they spent every day with, I don't think it's possible to understand. But I'm not trying to talk about James. What I'm trying to say is that I think I'm ready."

The glimmer of hope was alive again with her words.

She continued, "I think James would have wanted me to find someone. I even think he would be happy that it is you."

The lump in Pete's throat betrayed the emotion he felt at her words. "He was my friend, too," he said solemnly.

"I know."

They rode in silence for a few miles. Pete didn't know what to say, so he waited. Eventually, Jan spoke again. "I'm ready to date again, Pete. And I would really like that date to be you."

He reached over with his right hand and clasped hers, his eyes still on the road as they took the exit for Freedom. It was fitting, it seemed, to make the turn toward Freedom at the same time his heart moved ever closer to complete entanglement with hers.

Soon, he parked in front of Jan's cottage-style house, tucked in the trees. "I'll walk you in," he said.

Pete opened her door and they walked slowly to the porch. The moonlight peeked through the tall timbers of the evergreen trees, and the cool October night was still and clear.

"Good night, Janet." He leaned down and brushed his lips against her cheek. "I'll see you at church."

She nodded wordlessly, her fingers finding her

cheek. Apparently, Jan was as affected by his presence as he was by hers. He smiled to himself as he walked back to the car. He turned back as he reached the driver's side and saw Jan still motionless on the porch.

"Go inside, my dear."

Pete watched until she closed the door behind her. Once he knew she was safe, he climbed in his car, whistling with satisfaction.

Whatever Victoria had been talking about, he wasn't going to get worked up about it. This was just another exaggerated tale. And he wasn't going to let it ruin things with Jan.

5

With one last glance in the mirror to check her lipstick, Jan stepped out of her car and headed inside Freedom Bible Church. She was especially jittery this morning, and she hadn't even had coffee yet. Instead, her nervous energy about seeing Pete this morning had given her all the pep she needed.

Their date had ended well. It didn't make sense for her to be nervous, but she was. Part of her still thought maybe Pete would change his mind or decide she wasn't worth the hassle. A widow of nearly sixty came with baggage. The grief of a husband gone too soon. A child. A grandchild.

Pete had none of those things warring for his attention. Would he be happier with someone as unattached as himself?

Jan caught sight of her reflection in the glass door and shook off the doubt. Whatever God had in store for her—with or without Pete or any other man—she was ready for it.

Pete had beaten her in this morning and was already making the first jumbo pot of coffee when she stepped behind the counter with him.

"Good morning," she said.

He carefully dumped the scoop of coffee grounds into the basket before glancing at her with a crooked grin. "It's a great morning, I'd say." He winked at her, and though her head said his antics were "too much," her heart said "just right."

"A great day, hmm? What's so great about it?"

Pete slid the basket into the coffee maker and flipped the switch. Then he turned to her and stepped closer. "Well, for one, I get to see you."

Jan felt herself blush with pleasure.

He continued, "And two, it's a great day because God made it and allowed me to enjoy it."

Jan grinned at his cheerfulness this morning. He was always in a good mood, but this was another level. Had he spent the last thirty-six hours on cloud nine like she had? When Aiden and Jo had picked up Landon this morning, Jan had gotten so distracted by a daydream that her son had asked her what was going on. She ended up blaming her inattentiveness on the baby, even though he had actually slept through the night.

"I wanted to say that I had a really good time Friday night," she said. His silver eyes, reflecting the morning sunshine through the lobby windows, were on hers.

Pete took her hand gently. "I did too." He opened his mouth, but closed it without saying anything. He glanced around the lobby before releasing her hand. "We should probably get the food set up."

Jan felt the frustration rising. What had he been about to say? It wasn't that lame comment about the food. She glanced around and noticed the same thing he had. People were starting to arrive at the church and trickle into the lobby. Pete was right; they did need to get set up. She sighed. There would be another time to have the conversation.

Jan nodded at him and grabbed the boxes of pastries from behind the counter and carried them to the table out front. Pete nudged her with his hip as he brought over napkins and serving trays.

Before long, the coffee bar area was filled with churchgoers. She stood next to Pete as Heath walked up, a serious looking man with dark hair next to him. Jan recognized MacGuyver Spark—he'd lived in Freedom for a long time. Her heart had broken for him when his fiancée died.

She greeted him. "Good morning, gentlemen."

"Good to see you," Pete added.

Heath smiled at each of them. "Morning Jan. Pete." He shook Pete's hand then gestured to the man next to him. "You remember Mac, right? He took over as the head of security at the resort last year. I'm still not convinced he ever leaves, actually."

Mac reached out his hand to Pete. "Nice to see you, Pete."

Mac smiled, but it didn't reach his eyes. She saw the familiar look of aimlessness and loss that she'd seen so often in the mirror. She was glad he was here this morning. Freedom was a good place to heal. And Freedom Bible Church was a big part of that for her.

Heath, Mac, and Pete were off on a discussion about the lodge and the pros and cons of the tourist season. The calendar would soon read November and the ski runs had opened last weekend. Jan had debated purchasing her season lift pass this year. Each year, it seemed she used it less and less and took longer to recover each time she did. But nothing beat the feeling of flying down the mountain over fresh powder.

She excused herself from their conversation to check on the coffee supplies. When the music started inside the worship center and most of the lobby emptied, Pete came up next to her.

"It's nice to see Mac here. He's had a hard run."

Jan nodded. "Sandy was a lovely girl. Aiden worked with her at the firehouse. The whole department was shaken when she died."

Pete murmured his sorrow. "It was good to catch up with them about the Lodge. Did you hear they opened a new ski run?"

"It's been all the buzz around the shop. People around here sure love to ski."

Pete chuckled. "Sometimes, I feel like that's a prerequisite for living in Freedom. Jenny at the post office asks you before she'll file your change of address form and all."

The smile spread across her face in an instant. Pete always made her laugh with a quick joke. "I still love it, so I guess I'm safe. I was just thinking about whether I should get a season pass this year."

"We should go. I haven't been in a while either, but it would be fun to hit the slopes."

The last few times she'd gone, it had been with Aiden. She loved to watch him snowboard, though she usually prayed the entire time since he insisted on finding every jump on the run. Aiden didn't like to take many breaks either. It would be fun to go with someone who took things a little slower.

"That sounds really fun. Maybe I can take off during the week one day so we can miss the worst of the crowds." Folks from the city tended to overrun the mountain on the weekends, especially early in the season. Later in the season it was even worse, as the holiday travel crowd came out as well.

It didn't really matter. Jan knew, even if she and Pete spent most of the day waiting in line, it would be the highlight of her week.

6

Pete was excited when he picked up Jan on Wednesday morning. "Good morning! Ready to hit the slopes?" He grabbed her gear and placed it in the back of his truck. Tomorrow was the last day of October, and Jan needed to be at work for all the trick-or-treaters doing Halloween on the Square. The Harvest festival was the first weekend in November, which meant it started on Friday.

Today would be a great day for skiing though. Pete knew the resort staff had been hard at work creating the base layer of compacted artificial snow that would carry them through the early part of the season until more snow could fall. It helped that Aiden was on staff at the resort as a snowboarding instructor and always knew the condition of the slopes. He'd confirmed that they were in good shape. In fact, he even had some lessons booked.

Jan climbed into the truck. "I'm always a little nervous the first time I go out each year. How much has my body aged since last March?"

Pete chuckled. "I know what you mean. We'll start slow."

Jan nodded. "That sounds great. I'm pretty sure Aiden doesn't know that word when it comes to snow sports."

When they arrived at Freedom Ridge Resort fifteen minutes later, they carried their skis to the large open seating area at the base of the chair lifts. It wasn't far from the main portion of the resort, which made it easy to take a break inside to grab lunch, coffee, or just sit by the fire in the lodge.

Growing up in Freedom, Pete had been a skier most of his life. It had even come in handy a few times overseas, allowing him to fit right in at some of the most exclusive ski resorts in the Swiss Alps. The rich and powerful made valuable intelligence assets.

There was a special place in his heart for the Colorado Rockies, though. They took their place on the two-seat lift and began their ascent.

Pete looked at Jan once they were both settled. "Should we start off slow and get off at the midway stop?" The more difficult trails started higher up the mountain, and skiers could exit the chair lift halfway up to access the trails rated green and below.

"That sounds good. I don't think we need to tackle Liberty Run today, do you?" Jan chuckled, referring to the most difficult Black Diamond trail on the mountain.

"I'd lie and say I didn't care about impressing you, but I also don't think you'd be impressed to see me fall down the mountain and rescued by Ski Patrol."

Jan's laughter was exactly what he needed. All week, he had been stressing about Victoria's presence at the insurance dinner, wondering what she was talking about.

As they slowly climbed the mountain, he and Jan were in their own little world, with a view that was hard to beat. At higher elevations, the snow-capped rocky peaks flashed bright reflections from the sun, and below them, the trees rose in wide swaths from the snowy and stony ground, their continuous expanse broken only by the various trails of white snow cutting down the mountain.

At the midway point, they skied off the chair lift and moved out of the way of people who might get off behind them. Pete glanced at the signs, trying to decide which run he'd like to make. "What do you think? Independence or Patriot?" They were both intermediate slopes, but Pete knew they were quite different.

Jan didn't hesitate in her answer. "Patriot is my favorite. Let's start there." They followed the blue square trail signs to the right toward the Patriot trail. Scattered groups of skiers filled the area, seated on the snow, sitting on the various benches and tables, or teaching younger children.

At the top of the crest, they both lowered their goggles. The freshly-groomed trail stretched before them, only a few tracks marring the small, straight ridges left by the snowcats. They slid unhurriedly through the yellow slow zone until they cleared the yellow fencing. Jan waved and he saw her smile as she called, "See you at the bottom!"

Pete let his eyes follow her bright-blue ski jacket for a moment, admiring the ease with which she glided on the snow. He glanced around to make sure he was clear of any other skiers, then pushed off himself and let the sensation of skating across the snow wash over him.

The corduroy pattern left by the grooming overnight sounded like a zipper under his skis as they scoured a track on the small ridges. He watched Jan descend the mountain ahead of him, eager to reunite with her at the bottom of the trail. When he found a comfortable speed, Pete allowed himself to admire the landscape and scanned the tree line for any early-morning wildlife. He was passed by a snowboarder on the left, a camera strapped to the front of his helmet. He never understood that. Did people really watch their own run again afterward?

There was something peaceful about the time spent heading down the mountain. No phone calls, no emails. It was just him and God and a special part of creation.

By the time Pete caught up with Jan at the landing, he was more relaxed than he'd been in a week. The way Jan's obvious joy made his smile broaden was only further confirmation that he was doing the right thing. Victoria was mistaken, and everything was fine.

"Wow, that was fantastic! What a peaceful run. It makes me never want to come on a Saturday again!"

Pete grinned. "I know what you mean. I think I only saw five other people during that whole run."

"Ready to go again?"

"Yeah, let's go all the way up to Big Bear Run and then take a break when we make it down." Big Bear was an intermediate trail that started near the top of the mountain, joining up with Little Bear Run on the bottom half.

"That sounds great."

They skied over to the other chair lift and climbed on for the long ride up the mountain.

A few minutes into the ride, Jan scooted closer. "I always forget how chilly it is up here in the wind."

He gladly wrapped his arm around her. "Guess

we will have to huddle together. I'm the same way. I'll be shivering up here and sweating by the time I get down the mountain."

They sat in silence for a moment before Jan spoke again. "It's really beautiful up here, isn't it?"

Pete nodded. "You know, I've been all over the world and I couldn't find a place that compared to Freedom."

Some people might hear that and think he was exaggerating, but Jan knew he had traveled extensively. Of course, he'd led her to believe it was just travel for vacations.

"I guess I'll take your word for it. I haven't been many places, but I love it here, so I suppose I haven't needed to."

"Where would you go if you could go anywhere?"

"Oh, that's a tough question." Jan paused while she considered. "Can I choose two?"

Pete chuckled. "Sure. We are dreaming, after all."

"I want to go to Israel someday. To walk where Jesus walked? I can't imagine there is anything like it."

"And the other?"

Jan ducked her head. "It's kind of crazy. But I want to go somewhere that is as far from my normal as possible. Thailand or India or maybe somewhere in Africa? I don't know exactly. I just know I want to experience something so radically different that I have an entirely new perspective." Jan couldn't explain it, and rationally she knew it was unlikely that she would experience that level of travel adventure.

Not like Pete had. She'd lost track of the places he'd mentioned traveling to. "What's the craziest place you've gone to?"

Pete laughed. "I called my mom once and told her I was in Mozambique. She had to pull out a map and find it."

Jan made a funny face. "I think *I* need to pull out a map and find it."

"It's right next to Zimbabwe, and it's the closest part of Africa to Madagascar."

"Wow." Jan was impressed, but also a little sad. What could a small-town grandma like herself offer Pete, who had lived on the coast and traveled the world?

Pete must have sensed the change in her mood. He leaned forward slightly to meet her eyes. "There is a reason I came back to Freedom. In all those places, I never found peace until I came home."

Jan relaxed. Pete did seem rather settled, with his business, his rental cabins, and his role in the men's ministry at church.

"I'm glad. They say not all who wander are lost, but it feels like it would be hard to live too long without roots somewhere."

The chair lift reached the end and Jan carefully set her skis on the exit ramp and stood up. They skied toward the entrance of Big Bear Run.

"Pete?"

They both turned at the sound of his name, and the Kizner family waved excitedly.

Jan smiled at the obvious enjoyment of the children. She searched Shelly's eyes for signs of the illness, but if she was in pain, she was hiding it well. She looked tired, but happy.

"I didn't know you all could ski," Jan said.

"Hah! We couldn't, but Pete here was kind enough to hook us up with a lesson from a nice young man who works here at the resort. We are all leaving with a new skill." He cupped a hand around one side of his mouth and stage whispered, "And I'm pretty sure Kaylie here is leaving with a pretty big crush on Aiden." He winked at his oldest daughter, who looked to be about fourteen and immediately turned a dark shade of scarlet.

"Dad, don't!"

Jan chuckled. "Don't worry about it, Kaylie. You aren't the first to fall for my son's charm."

"Aiden is your son?" The question came from Shelly.

Jan filled with pride. "He sure is. He'd be thrilled to hear you had a good lesson and that you are back on the mountain without him! If you leave a review on the resort's website, be sure to mention him by name. I guess that's how he gets bonuses and the like."

"We definitely will. We expected to enjoy the mountain and mostly hang out in the cabin, but the skiing definitely brought the trip to a whole other level. We wouldn't have tried it without your suggestion, Pete, so thank you."

"Happy to help. I'm so glad you've had a great trip."

As the family skied away, Jan considered Pete again. She had no idea he had arranged all that with Aiden. His generous heart never ceased to amaze her.

"That was a really kind thing you did."

Pete shrugged. "They needed a little push to do something memorable. I'm glad I was able to help. And Aiden was the one who donated his time, so I barely did anything."

"Still, you arranged it. And now they will always have that memory with their mom. That's a gift they will always cherish."

Pete smiled. "I hope so." Then he lowered his goggles and looked at the trail stretching before them.

Jan lowered her goggles and smiled mischievously at him. "Race you to the bottom? Loser buys lunch."

"Oh, you are trouble, Jan Clark."

She laughed. "So I've heard." Without waiting for a response, she pushed off and found the natural rhythm of side to side that would control her descent down the mountain. As long as she was physically able, Jan knew she wouldn't give this up. It felt a bit like flying, and there was nothing that compared. Plus, if she could enjoy the mountain with a handsome, funny man, it was all the better.

AT THE BOTTOM of the mountain, Pete slid his skis to a stop next to Jan, who had already pulled off her goggles and helmet.

"What took you so long, O'Rourke?" Her words were slightly breathless and full of laughter.

"I call interference. That whole group of children came out after the midway drop-off and it was like dodging potholes in April. You must have just missed them, because I had to slow way down." She laughed and Pete grew more adamant. "I'm serious. You never know what those little ones are going to do! It was hilarious to watch the little herd of tiny skiers, but I blame them solidly for my loss."

The little ones were fearless and had absolutely no concern that they might be in the way.

"Fair is fair. Bad luck and tiny obstacles aside, you still lost. I think a burger from Basecamp will totally hit the spot. They taste better as the spoils of victory."

Her gloating was good-natured and Pete couldn't help but join her in laughing. "Fine, fine. Let's go. I could use a bite. I forgot how hungry it makes you."

Lunch was a casual affair. Basecamp specialized in hearty food served fast. Despite their casual decor and the paper plates, Basecamp had the best burger on the mountain. Although, it was hotly debated if it was simply the skiing appetite that made it taste so good.

They dropped their skis off on the racks outside. Pete ordered at the counter while Jan found a spot at the end of one of the wooden communal tables that filled the large dining room. There were also outdoor tables, but Jan had suggested getting out of the sun for a bit.

By the end of the day, Pete was sure he wouldn't be able to walk for a week. It was worth it though. He hadn't enjoyed a day so thoroughly in as long as he could remember. He and Jan seemed to be perfectly in sync with when to take breaks, when to go quickly, and when to take a leisurely ski down an easy trail.

He loaded their skis in the back of his truck. "Want to grab dinner before I take you home?"

Jan laughed. "I'm starving, but I think I better just go home and clean up. Maybe Friday night at the Harvest Festival?"

"It's a date." And this time, it really was.

7

Jan wrapped the soft flannel scarf around her neck and tucked her hands in her pockets as she waited for Pete to get back from the food trucks with their dinner. The Harvest Festival in Freedom Ridge was no small affair. The streets were closed for the hay ride around the square, and there were booths with all kinds of games, like bobbing for apples and pumpkin chucking. A handful of local food trucks provided food for the event.

Jan watched with a smile as kids ran past, one chasing the rest with a handful of brown leaves. While she'd enjoyed seeing the kids dressed up last night as superheroes and princesses and a hundred other characters she didn't even recognize, she much preferred the Harvest festival to Halloween.

Pete brought back two plates. One heaping with French fries loaded with pulled pork, cheese, and jalapenos, and the other holding an assortment of small tacos.

"I hope this works. There were too many choices. I panicked and ordered the first two things I saw."

She laughed. "It looks amazing. Shorty's has the best BBQ, don't they?"

"Definitely."

They sat at the picnic table and ate their dinner. Then, after Pete had gathered all the empty containers and found a trash can, he offered her his hand. She slid her hand into his and couldn't help but feel like something else was sliding into place, too. Everything about the moment felt right.

They strolled through the festival, watching Derek and Aiden compete to see who could throw a pumpkin the farthest and chatting with friends.

Jan saw the Pembrokes coming toward them down the sidewalk and waved.

"Well, well, well. What have we here?" Art grinned and looked pointedly at their joined hands.

Her face flushed, despite the chill in the air.

Isabella chimed in as well. "It's about time, you two!"

She chuckled uncomfortably at her friend's comment. Maybe it had been a long time coming, but it was a big deal to her. Moving forward with someone wasn't an easy decision she could make quickly.

Pete shrugged. "We're ready now. That's all that matters."

She warmed at his response. Somehow, he knew exactly what to say. Perhaps he'd been ready to enter a relationship before her, but Pete had never pushed or been impatient. She was truly blessed to have him as a friend—and now, as more than that.

They said goodbye to the Pembrokes and headed toward the gazebo. He watched the children run with a smile on his face.

"Can I ask you a question?"

"Of course."

"I know you've never been married, but have you ever, you know, gotten close? You're a handsome man, good with kids… How come no woman ever snapped you up when you lived in Virginia?"

Pete continued watching the kids while he answered. "There was someone, once. I thought it might work, but she wasn't exactly the picket fence type."

A memory of the glamourous woman from the insurance dinner flashed.

He met her eyes and continued, "I think God knew it wasn't the right time for me."

Her heart stuttered at the implication. She had already admitted that the timing finally felt right for her. She'd been alone for ten years. Pete had been waiting for four times that. Did he really believe she was the one and this was the time?

For once, Jan was speechless.

But Pete didn't seem to require a response to the revelation he'd just dropped. "They're quite good," he commented casually about the music.

There was a quartet playing folk and gospel songs. While they stood and listened, Pete dropped her hand and tucked her close to his side instead, wrapping his arm around her. She leaned into the warmth and looked up at him with a smile. She couldn't imagine a more perfect end to a lovely week.

At church on Sunday morning, Jan waved to Patience Martel. She ran a bakery in Freedom and made the most delicious cakes and cupcakes. When she came over, Jan greeted her with a hug. "Good morning! How are you?" Patience was close in age to Aiden and Jan had known her family for years.

"I'm good. Actually, I'm swamped at the bakery. Seems like I've got a wedding every weekend, sometimes two!"

Jan smiled. "That's wonderful. The cake you made for Aiden and Jo's wedding was amazing. I told Addison to talk to you whenever Ty proposes," she added with a chuckle. The two were completely head over heels, so everyone knew it was only a matter of time.

"She mentioned it to me. I think she's already hearing wedding bells. That reminds me, I'm thinking about hiring an assistant. Know anyone looking?"

"Can't say that I do, but I'll keep my ears open."

"I appreciate it. No one knows everyone in Freedom the way you do," Patience said with a wink.

Jan laughed. It was true. She loved to talk with people, and since Stories and Scones had become kind of a community hub, she got the scoop more often than not.

Out of the corner of her eye, Jan saw a woman take her hand off the hot water carafe and move it to coffee instead. She got Pete's attention. "Would you check the hot water?"

"Sure thing," he replied with a smile. She saw his gaze move over her shoulder to somewhere across the room. His smile disappeared and his face went pale.

She turned to see if she could identify what he was looking at. All she saw was the normal flow of people in the front doors, lingering in the lobby and moving slowly into the worship center. Jan looked back at him. She was getting worried now. He looked like he had seen a ghost.

"Pete? Is everything okay?"

Her words seemed to startle him back into the conversation. "Huh? Oh, umm, I just... I need to check on something. Are you good here?" He gestured to the coffee bar.

Jan could tell he had already checked out. "I've got it."

"Great, thanks." His words were faded, since he was already three steps away as he spoke them.

What in the world?

She turned to Patience. "Sorry, duty calls."

"No problem. I'll see you around."

"Tell your parents I said hello." After Patience stepped away, Jan moved closer to the coffee table.

The elderly woman turned to her. "Excuse me, the decaf is empty. Do you have more?"

"Good morning! I sure do. I think it just finished brewing back here. Give me one minute."

Jan went through the motions of replacing the coffee pot, but her mind was on Pete. Where had he gone? Jan said a quick prayer that everything was okay. Whatever Pete had seen across the lobby, it had him acting really strange.

PETE'S HEART raced as he walked as quickly as he could across the church parking lot.

He barely registered it when Derek Held waved

at him as he and Megan walked toward the church. "Good morning, Pete!" Derek called.

Pete stumbled. He needed to reply. Stay in character. Except this wasn't an assignment. This was his life! "Hey Derek."

"How's it going?"

He was already moving. What had Derek said? He held a hand up in apology. "Sorry, can't chat." He infused his voice with carefree friendliness. "I'll see you later!"

As quickly as he could without seeming suspicious, he hustled away, his entire focus on getting out of there. Finally, he stopped at his truck, unsure what to do.

Had it really been…? No. That was impossible. But when he combined the presence of Victoria at the insurance dinner with the sight of Ian Knight, perhaps it wasn't such a crazy leap after all.

But Ian Knight was dead. Pete had seen the helicopter go down himself.

So why was a dead man walking around Freedom?

After a cursory check under the truck for explosives, Pete opened the back door on the driver's side and unlatched the hidden compartment there. He glanced around the parking lot to make sure he wasn't being watched before pulling out a holster and strapping it to his shoulder under his coat. Then he grabbed the handgun, checked the safety, and slid it into place.

Whatever was happening, Pete was going to be ready. As much as he wanted to go back and see Jan, he knew he needed to see if he had really seen what he thought or if he was just hallucinating.

Maybe he had a brain tumor.

At this point, perhaps that would be preferable to the idea that Ian Knight was alive and looking for Pete.

He drove the three blocks to the office instead of going home. He needed to find answers, and he needed them quickly. If Knight really was alive and wanted to talk to him, Pete knew exactly how the former member of MI6 would reach out.

Looking both ways down the street, and with an instinctual glance at the rooftops for snipers, Pete unlocked his office and stepped inside. For years after leaving the agency, it had been as natural as breathing to do a site evaluation like that every time he went somewhere. But he hadn't felt the need to do it in years. He hated that he felt the need to do it now. Pete locked the door behind him and crossed to his personal office in the back.

Once his laptop was fired up, Pete opened the browser and typed in the IP address for the secure mailbox he'd used while he was an agent. It wasn't agency supplied, but sometimes a spy needed to talk

Believing the Hero

off the record with contacts. Or, in this case, his counterparts in foreign agencies.

The email address had been active but mostly unmonitored for the better part of ten years. Only fourteen messages remained unread. A few notes from contacts around the world, mostly in the year after he retired. He ignored those. The messages at the very top were what he wanted.

Sent three days ago.

Sender: KnightEye

Pete read the message from start to finish, then read it again. And again.

It's been a long time, David. I have some questions, and you have the answers. I need to meet with you. I'll be in touch.

Another message, yesterday.

Another message, 10 minutes ago.

You know you can't run away. I won't let you go. Not until I have what I want.

Pete's stomach dropped.

Ian didn't say what he wanted here, probably paranoid, and perhaps rightfully so. He wanted to meet.

Pete didn't know what to do. One thing was certain, though. Nothing good could come from meeting with Ian Knight. He shut the laptop and leaned back in the soft leather office chair, covering his face with his hands. Pete wasn't one to utter curse words, but at that moment, he was sorely tempted.

The phone rang on his desk.

Pete stared at the blinking red light. No one in Freedom would be calling at 9:45 on a Sunday morning. It could only mean one thing.

Knight had watched him leave the church and seen him come to the office. The phone continued ringing. Instead of saying the swear word on the tip of his tongue, Pete prayed out loud. "I need you, Jesus."

Then he took a deep breath and answered the call.

8

The next day, Pete checked over his shoulder and opened the door to the Freedom City Library. The library was several blocks from downtown, close to the high school.

"Hey, Pete, what brings you in?"

Pete waved casually at Wendy, the quiet librarian with thick-framed glasses.

"Just need to grab a couple books. Never know when we'll get snowed in," he said with a laugh. "Remember that doozy a couple years back?" Deflection was a skill he'd perfected during his service.

Wendy nodded. "I was stuck here at the library for two days."

It was taking every ounce of restraint Pete had to continue the polite conversation instead of locating the dead drop location Knight had given him on the phone.

"Wow. I hope you keep a stash of food here!"

She chuckled. "I do now. At least we had a vending machine."

"Well that's good! I'll see you in a while," he ended the conversation. Perhaps it was abrupt, but his patience was running short today.

Pete went to the non-fiction section, the string of numbers running through his head.

"Are you a fan of Japanese Architecture?" Knight's tone had been mocking. He was having far too much fun with this.

"What?"

"728.3, Pete," Knight had said.

To anyone else, it was nonsense. But it had given Pete exactly the information he needed to pick up whatever it was that Knight had left for him.

It was an old trick, one they'd used a half dozen times in cities around the world. Just a short string of numbers, and the other person could pinpoint the drop. At least to within a book or two.

Pete trailed his finger along the spines, counting up with the numbers printed on little white labels. 718. 722. 728. There. *The Lesson of Japanese Architecture.*

Pete pulled the book out and thumbed the pages until a small sheet of paper fell out. It was a copy of a birth certificate. Pete read the name and his heart dropped into his stomach.

Ariana Voltoro. Born twenty-two years ago in Italy as the only child of Antonio Voltoro. Yes, that Voltoro. When Pete helped take down Tony V., he had also been the one to discover the twelve-year-old daughter Antonio had successfully hidden from the world. Friends and foes alike, no one knew the notorious arms dealer had a daughter.

Pete felt sorry for the girl. After all, no one got to choose their parents. At least Tony had provided a hefty trust fund for her future. Pete rolled his eyes. He might have been a ruthless criminal, but Tony V. had loved his daughter. But she was lucky that her father hadn't gotten her killed—or worse—by double-crossing the wrong person. Tony had been right to keep her hidden.

And Pete was determined to do the same. He had called in every favor he was owed to get the girl a new identity and adopted into an American family. They had no idea of her true parentage. Pete had made sure that every trace of Ariana's existence had been wiped out. So how did Ian get his hands on this?

And why?

He skimmed the next paper—a bank statement—from the small stack, and the pieces started falling into place. Someone had taken over the family business. But they apparently weren't nearly as enterprising as the former boss. The Voltoros were in trouble. And they needed Ariana's trust fund to prop up the business.

They'd never find her on their own, though. And Pete definitely wasn't going to help them.

So where did that leave him?

To maintain appearances, Pete grabbed a few novels from the fiction shelves before checking out and heading back to his truck.

Once he climbed inside, he called his friend, Heath. Heath owned a security firm based in Freedom, but more than that, Heath shared his background in intelligence. If anyone would be able to talk through this, it was him.

"This is Heath."

"Hey, man, it's Pete. You got a minute?"

"Yeah, of course. What do you need?"

Pete appreciated the way Heath cut to the chase and didn't waste time with small talk. "I've got a bit of a conundrum," Pete said casually, though it was the understatement of the century. "I wanted your thoughts."

"Okay, shoot."

Pete debated how to approach this. "Let's say someone from your past, someone who knows that you *know* things… Let's say, hypothetically, they show up in Freedom and demand you provide intel."

"Pete..." Heath's tone held a warning. His friend obviously didn't like where this was going.

"I know," Pete said, "just go with me here."

"Hypothetically, huh?" The sarcasm dripped in Heath's voice.

"Mm-hmm."

"Well, *hypothetically*, I would go to the police."

Pete wasn't surprised there. "Okay. And if there is nothing they can do?"

"Is everything okay, Pete?"

"It's fine. It's nothing serious. Just... Say a prayer for me, all right?"

"Of course. I guess I would do everything I had to do to protect my family, my town, and the intel. First things first, I'd get ahead of it. Get the people I love out of harm's way before anything went down." Heath's answer wasn't surprising. After falling in love last year with the local artist, Claire, Heath was even more territorial than he'd been before. The answer got Pete's wheels turning, though. "If there is something going on, you can tell me. You know I've got your six, right?"

Pete chuckled, despite the heaviness of the conversation. "Oh, is that why you call it that?" referring to the name of Heath's security firm: Got Your Six.

"I'm serious," Heath said.

"I know. Thanks, man."

Jan didn't see Pete again until Wednesday. His daily visits to Stories and Scones stopped, and she even walked down to his office on Tuesday, just to be told he was out.

This was very unusual. Sure, Pete liked to travel and go camping, but he'd never gone without notice.

He didn't exactly owe her an explanation. They weren't really in a relationship, right? But didn't friends usually try to say something before falling off the face of the earth?

On Wednesday, she stopped by his office again.

"Is he here?" she asked Tessa, his receptionist.

"I'm here," Pete's voice came from the back office. The door was cracked and Jan slipped past Tessa's desk and pushed her way in.

He was sick. That was the only explanation for the gray pallor of his skin, the bags under his eyes, and the wrinkled shirt that was so counter to his usual sharp appearance.

"Oh my goodness, Pete. What's wrong?"

His close-lipped smile didn't meet his eyes. "It's nothing. Just dealing with some stuff."

Jan tried not to roll her eyes. Typical man, never willing to share. Still, he was her friend. Wasn't he even more than that now?

"Is there anything I can do?"

Pete shook his head. "No. Actually, I wanted to talk to you. I know we had been talking about..." He waved his hand through the air. "You know. Us."

Jan felt her blood pressure rise. She did know. She'd been so excited about the possibility. After all the years mourning James, she finally felt like there was the potential for her to love someone again.

She swallowed the thick lump in her throat and nodded.

"I just don't think it's a good idea," Pete finished.

The sting of unsheathed tears burned behind her eyes. It had been decades since she felt the barb of rejection from a man, and she was definitely not interested in it becoming a regular occurrence.

She stuck out her chin and pressed her lips together. "If that's what you want, I won't argue."

"Are...are we still friends?"

She was surprised at the worry in Pete's voice. Her hurt resolve softened. "Of course, Petey."

He relaxed at her response. "I'll see you at the shop tomorrow," he said.

She nodded and turned back to the door. Everything she'd been looking forward to had changed in an instant. Not this one, though. It had changed whenever Pete saw whatever he had seen at church on Sunday morning. There was something more going on, but if Pete wasn't going to let her in, she wasn't going to push.

Jan had enough good, uncomplicated things in her life. Landon. The coffee shop. Aiden and Joanna. Her women's studies at church. She just needed to focus on those and forget about whatever almost could have happened with Pete, or any other man.

Dating at her age was a foolish thought, anyway.

Pete put on his game face and walked inside the church. He hadn't seen or heard from Knight again, but it was only a matter of time. It wasn't Ian he was worried about this morning, though. Seeing Jan would be the truest test of his acting ability.

Turning her away at his office had been the hardest thing to do, but it was for the best. He had no business getting her involved in any of this. As much as he wanted to pursue her, he needed Jan to be safe.

His visits to Stories and Scones had been stilted and uncomfortable. But for the sake of normalcy, Pete needed to keep going. It would get easier, right? And conversations at the coffee shop were short and shallow by nature. This morning at church though? They'd be together at the coffee bar for at least forty-five minutes. If his time at Stories and Scones this week was any indication, they would run out of topics to discuss within the first five.

"Good morning, Janet."

The way her eyes widened told him he should have stuck with Jan. Her friends called her Jan. Janet felt...intimate.

"Morning, Petey."

There was a pleasant slice of normalcy in the way she teased him with his nickname.

"Did you have a good Saturday?" There. That was a safe topic. Unless she went on a date or something. He frowned. Would she have had a date already?

Her eyes lit up. "Oh yes. I took Landon for the afternoon. It was a treat to watch him laugh as I blew bubbles for him. Of course, now my kitchen floor is all sticky, but that'll clean."

Jan carried such pure joy within her. What would it be like to share in that? Pete had faith. He even had confidence in Christ. But even before Knight showed up unexpectedly, it was as though the shadows of his past always cast a heaviness over things. How was Jan, with her losses, able to live with such fullness of joy?

He smiled broadly at her obvious happiness, stepping closer. "That sounds fun. He's a fun kid."

"He is. I'm lucky to have him. When Aiden and Joanna got together, it was an answer to prayer. He needed her."

"Men need a good woman in their life to keep them in line." Pete felt the heat at his collar when he registered his words. He'd spoken them unthinking about the double meaning.

Jan didn't miss it. Her eyebrows raised. "Even you?"

He cleared his throat. "Especially me. Look, Jan… I'm sorry it didn't work out." He grabbed her hands. "I care about you a great deal. I've just got some stuff going on."

Pete hated the shimmer of moisture in her eyes. Hurting Jan was never supposed to happen. Better it happened now than when they'd gotten more serious, right?

He pulled her in for a hug, soaking in the feeling of wrapping her in his arms. Ignoring how much it pained him to know he wouldn't do this again. Not like this, with his heart still on the line.

Jan took a deep breath and pulled back. He gently released her.

"We should prep the coffee," she said.

Pete nodded. Yeah, he supposed they should. Even if all he wanted was to continue holding her. He prayed for wisdom while he moved muffins from the plastic containers onto the serving trays. In his days as an agent, he hadn't turned to God as often as he should have. And he had the bad decisions haunting him to prove it.

If there was anything that could make this situation with Knight end well, it was praying about it.

9

Jan took a deep breath before knocking on Pete's front door. She'd been here before, once or twice for a prayer meeting. A few times with James for dinner. But never alone.

The door swung open, revealing Pete in a pullover sweater and jeans, a confused look on his face.

His eyes darted to the left and right down the street. "Jan, what's going on? Is everything okay?" Before he let her answer, Pete was ushering her inside. He shut the door behind her.

"No, everything is not fine, Pete."

His eyes widened. "What happened?"

Jan frowned. Were men really that clueless? She'd

almost forgotten. "What happened? You happened! I was perfectly content, Pete. I was happy with my little coffee shop and my grandson and my church friends. I was happy with our friendship." Pete's face revealed nothing. Her frustration bubbled over. "And then you went and—" she whipped her finger in a spiral, "—stirred everything up."

This overly-emotional outburst was not like her. She took a deep breath and continued with a calmer voice. "Pete. I'm too old for this. I don't want to play games with you. I want to be with you. For the first time, I feel as though I found someone to call a partner again."

Pete's eyes softened and he sighed. "Jan, I can't—"

"Oh, stop it, Pete. Give me one good reason you can't! And if you say you don't feel the same way as I do, I'm calling malarkey."

A smile broke through the stoic facade of Pete's face, but he didn't say anything.

Jan pushed a little further. "Do you? Feel the same way?"

Pete pressed his fingers to his eyes and he groaned. "Argh. Yes, Janet. Of course I do. I've been trying to show you how I felt for a while now." He moved closer to her spot on the couch and grabbed her fingers.

Hope blossomed deep in her chest again, and she

tried to tamp it down. She'd been here before with Pete.

"So what, then? What is the problem?" The frustration was simmering again.

Pete's fingers were warm on hers. She stared at their interlocked fingers before looking back to his kind eyes.

"Janet, there is nothing in the world I want more than to be with you and build a future with you. We might not be teenagers, but we've got a lot of good years left. And I'd really like to spend them together."

Pete was saying all the right words. But she could hear the unspoken 'but' at the end of his declaration. "Why do you keep pulling back, then?"

Pete sighed. "Do you trust me?" His eyes pleaded with her.

If he'd asked her that two weeks ago, the answer would have been an unqualified yes. Did she still, despite the hurt feelings of the recent past? "Yes."

His smile of relief was instantaneous. "I don't deserve you, Jan Clark. But I'm not going to let that stop me. I can't tell you everything. But I promise… this isn't me saying we can't be together. I just need some time."

She tried to focus on the things he'd said that she liked. He had feelings for her. He wanted a future together. But he couldn't tell her why it wouldn't work right now.

"Why?"

He looked her in the eye, and his voice dropped low and quiet. "I'll tell you when I can. Do you believe me?"

Jan's eyes fell closed. "Yes," she whispered, then looked back at him.

Pete squeezed her fingers, then he leaned close. He brought one hand up to cradle her face, and Jan leaned into the contact as he lowered his lips to hers. The kiss was soft and warm, and the foreign feeling of his mouth on hers was both exhilarating and impossibly familiar. Kissing Pete was like coming home, yet entirely new.

Pete broke the kiss and laid his forehead against hers. "I promise to tell you when I can."

"I promise to trust you."

"O'Rourke, don't underestimate me." Even through the phone, Ian Knight's voice was as cold as New Year's Eve night in the mountains.

No, Pete would never underestimate Knight. But he also would never help him destroy the life of an innocent child. Ariana might be twenty-seven years old now, but he would always see her as the doe-eyed twelve-year-old whose hand he had held as they flew across the ocean to her new life.

"I could say the same to you, Knight. I don't know what you think you have, but if Tony V. had a daughter, she's long gone." Pete sounded matter-of-fact in his assertion.

"Don't lie to me!" Knight's outburst was uncharacteristic of the cool operator from Pete's past. Was there something else going on? Ian's next words were measured. "I know you can help me find her."

Pete's jaw tightened. "Even if that were the case, the truth is that I wouldn't help you. What kind of man do you think I am?" Knight couldn't force anything out of him. Pete had been tortured before. He knew he wouldn't break.

Ian's dark chuckle made the hair stand up on Pete's neck. "Don't forget, David. I know exactly what kind of man you are. I was there in Rome. Remember?"

His fingernails dug into his palms at the shameful reminder. He couldn't go there. Pete knew he'd made mistakes. But he also knew that God had forgiven him. That was more than enough. "Perhaps you knew me then. But you don't know me now."

"Oh, but I think I do. I know everything there is to know about you, Petey." Pete's eyes widened. "Don't believe me? While you're at your little Bible study tonight," Ian sneered at the words, "check under the first row. I left you a little present."

The line dropped and Pete scrambled into gear.

Waiting until tonight wasn't an option. Knight had clearly lost it, and who knew what sort of "present" the man was referring to. It could be a bomb, for all Pete knew.

He debated calling Pastor Justin and clearing the building, just in case. How would he explain that one? Instead, Pete drove to the church, making sure he wasn't being followed. He used his key to enter through a side entrance and walked through the dimly lit worship center toward the front row.

The flashlight on his phone cast shadows around the large space as he knelt down to look. There. A flash of orange caught his eye. The manila envelope was taped to the bottom of the pew. Pete used the light to make sure he hadn't missed anything else before removing the envelope. He tucked it under his arm and made his way out of the church.

Once he was back in his truck, Pete unfolded the clasp and slid the papers out of the envelope. The blood drained from his face as the contents registered. Photos. Dozens of photos of Jan and him. At the coffee shop, at church, at the insurance board dinner. And the other night, at his house. His palm cradled her face, and the intimacy of the moment was perfectly captured in the black-and-white image. If it wasn't for the windowpane making it obvious the image was caught by a surveillance unit, it would make a romantic shot.

As it was, though, the sight made Pete's blood run cold.

The last image was of Jan's house. She stood on the step with Landon on her hip, as Aiden and Joanna walked toward the camera.

It was as clear a threat as he had ever seen. If Pete didn't help Knight, the rogue agent would target Jan and her family. It was his worst nightmare. This was exactly why an agent never got to have a life, a family. It made them vulnerable. Weak. It made *him* vulnerable. He knew that he would give Ian anything the monster wanted if Jan was in danger.

Pete went back inside the church, this time through the front door. He took a seat in the same dim sanctuary and prayed for wisdom. Never in his life had Pete prayed so hard.

When the lights flipped on, Pastor Justin stepped inside. "Oh, I didn't know anyone was here."

Pete looked back. "Hey, Pastor." He could hear the defeat in his own voice.

"Pete, what's going on? You're awfully early for men's group. It doesn't start for—" Justin checked his watch, "—two more hours."

Pete attempted a smile, but it was a weak effort. "I just needed some uninterrupted time with the Lord."

"Don't we all," Pastor Justin said. "Anything I can help with?"

Pete needed help, but he didn't think the young Pastor had the particular skills he needed. "I'd appreciate your prayers, sir." He knew he had an ally in the Lord. But he also needed an earthly ally. He had to assume his phone was tapped, but he had to reach out to Heath. He looked up at Justin. "Oh, and can I borrow your cell phone?"

JAN BUILT a block tower with Landon for the thirtieth time, waiting for him to decide it was tall enough to knock down this time. The little boy shrieked with laughter each time, and Jan couldn't help but smile at his enthusiasm.

"Okay, Landon James. One more time and then it's time for pajamas."

She braced herself for a meltdown, but Landon cooperated without complaint. She got him dressed, brushed his teeth, and read him a Bible story. Then she brushed the hair back from his forehead and kissed him.

"Good night, sweet boy. Gigi loves you!"

"Nigh nigh," came the drowsy reply.

She loved this precious child more than anything in the entire world. If asked, she'd give up everything for him. It was especially meaningful to her that Aiden and Jo had chosen to honor Aiden's father with Landon's middle name. Every time she said his full name, it was a little reminder that James lived on in their memories. But it was also a reminder that he was gone.

And even seven years later, that never got easier.

James had been a daredevil. He and Aiden loved to chase that adrenaline high. Firefighting had catered right to that need. James had said more than once that there was nothing like fighting a live one. Still, she'd always figured it would be the rock climbing or the sky diving or the white water rafting that would get him. Not his day job.

When she'd gone to Pete's house, she hadn't known what to expect. As much as she cared for Pete, he would never replace James. Knowing that he understood that was important.

And admitting to him that she had real feelings was a big step. They'd been in limbo since the insurance dinner, and she was tired of all the uncertainty.

Whatever was going on with Pete, she had to trust him. She had no idea what it could possibly be, though. It wasn't like Pete to keep secrets. He'd asked her to trust him, but didn't he trust her?

Jan sighed as she picked up the blocks and said a prayer for their relationship. If you could call this hot-and-cold whiplash a relationship. Still, she had said she would trust Pete. But more importantly, she was trusting God.

Despite the strange emotional rollercoaster, she still felt God had a hand in this. Everything she knew about Pete told her that he was honest and good. So until something told her otherwise, she would just have to be patient.

10

Pete unlocked the cabin and disarmed the state-of-the-art security system. Heath would be here any minute, and Pete would finally get to lay everything out in the open. He had maintained every precaution—calling Heath from Pastor Justin's phone and borrowing Art's car to be sure he wasn't tailed to the safe house.

He had to believe the security of the safe house had not been compromised. The alternative was... unsettling. But he'd been careful when he set up this property, running it through a completely unrelated shell corporation. His name was nowhere to be found, no matter how deep in the weeds someone went.

Heath already knew about its existence, due to a little trouble last year for Claire. Or at least, they had thought it was about Claire. Either way, Heath had made use of the safe house and its strategic defensive position. It held the high ground. The natural defense coupled with the high-tech security system including solar-powered motion sensors and cameras with night vision made the cabin a fortress if needed.

He glanced around the simple room. The front door opened into a small living area, with a kitchen and bathroom behind. A small table separated the spaces, and a staircase led to the loft and the only bed.

At 700 square feet, it certainly didn't look like a fortress, but he knew the rustic cabin held a few secrets. After all, he'd hidden them himself. He started a fire, but didn't bother with the heat. This meeting wouldn't last long.

Pete's shoulders tensed as his phone chimed with an alert from the security application. Motion sensors on the road. Heath was here. Pete peeked through the curtain to be certain, not quite relaxing until he confirmed it was Heath who stepped down from the large SUV.

He opened the door. "Hey. Thanks for coming."

"Anytime, seriously."

"Come on in, and I'll tell you what I'm dealing with." Pete stepped to the side to let his friend inside.

"It's strange to be back," Heath said. "A lot of

memories in place. Some of the best, and some that make my blood run cold." He looked back toward the road and rubbed his shoulder.

Pete remembered how things had come to a head last year. "I'll bet. I'm glad to have this place. But I'm also glad I've never spent much time here."

"So why are we here now?" There he went, cutting to the chase again.

Pete hesitated. He took a deep breath. "Do you mind if I pray first?"

Heath nodded and bowed his head. Pete said a quick prayer, expressing his thanks for his friend and asking God to give them both wisdom as they discussed the issue at hand.

"Amen," Heath echoed when Pete finished.

"Okay, here's the deal. A few weeks ago, someone I used to work with at MI6 showed up at the Insurance dinner in Denver. She warned me that someone was looking for me, but we ran out of time to finish the conversation." Pete realized he hadn't heard anything else from Victoria. She'd said she would be around. Was she still?

"There is an agent. An ex-agent for MI6—Ian Knight. I worked with him back in the day, but he was a real piece of work. He would do anything to complete a job. And apparently, he went rogue. He reached out to me, and he wants intel."

"What kind of intel?"

"The kind I can't give." Heath's eyebrows jumped at Pete's words. Pete sighed. He had to trust Heath. If he couldn't, there was no hope. "There was a girl—the daughter of an arm's dealer. No one knew she existed." Pete swallowed. "I was the one who found her after her father was eliminated. She was twelve, Heath. And the Agency didn't even care if she lived through the hit. I pulled every favor I had to get her a new life and bury her old one. As far as anyone else was concerned, Ariana Voltoro died that day. But she got a new life."

Heath listened intently. "That was a good thing you did, Pete."

Pete just shook his head. He hadn't done it for the accolades. No one was ever supposed to know. "She's twenty-seven now. Lives in Phoenix, last I checked. And Ian Knight knows she isn't dead. He wants her, and he thinks I'm the way he's going to find her."

Heath's hands were steepled under his chin. "Okay. Let me think."

"There's more," Pete said. "I told him no. Then he sent me this." Pete slid the manila envelope over to Heath. Unable to look at the photos again, or even watch Heath's expression as he saw them, Pete stood and paced the small cabin.

Heath swore under his breath. "When did you get this?"

"Yesterday. I called you right away. Jan cannot get pulled into this." Pete turned back toward the sofa. "I need your help."

"Anything you need. Even if you hadn't saved my tail last year, you're my friend, Pete. You're not alone on this one."

How had Heath known exactly what Pete needed to hear? Too many times, Pete had been on his own in a foreign country with no safety net. He knew from experience that he couldn't control all the variables if he was on his own.

"Thanks, man. Here's what I'm thinking." Pete detailed a plan that would have Ian playing right into his hand. And Ariana would be completely safe.

"What about Jan?" Heath asked.

"I don't know. I want to bring her here. I'm not sure if she'll listen to me, though. Things are a little...strained right now."

Heath quirked an eyebrow but didn't say anything.

He gestured to the photo face up on the table of he and Jan mid-kiss. "Obviously, we have feelings for each other. But just when I thought we were finally going to try it out, this whole situation came up. I've been trying to keep her at arms' length ever since."

"And how's that working for you?" Heath asked dryly.

"Yeah, yeah. I get it. Maybe you can help convince

her if she won't listen to me? Jan can be a bit stubborn."

Heath chuckled. "Yeah, I can do that. We should probably get Aiden, Jo, and their boy up here, too."

Pete nodded. "Good idea. Maybe Jan will be more willing to hideout if it is protecting her family."

They finished discussing the details and the timing. Heath looked at the threatening photo again. "You okay if I bring Adam in? Need-to-know, maybe?" Adam was Heath's partner. Pete only knew him casually, but if Heath trusted the man, Pete was on board.

"Need-to-know," Pete confirmed. Adam didn't have to know exactly why this man was coming after Jan, just that they were going to protect her.

After they wrapped up, Pete put out the fire and armed the security system before locking the cabin. The gravel drive crunched under their shoes as they walked out to their vehicles.

"Thanks again," Pete said. His words didn't begin to convey the gratitude he felt.

Heath clapped a heavy hand on his shoulder. "We'll get this guy, okay?"

Pete nodded. They had to get him. There was no other option.

JAN WENT to church on Sunday, excited and a little nervous to see Pete again. She'd decided to trust him —and God. But which Pete would she get today? The charming, warm man who made her blush and dream of evenings together on the porch swing? Or the secretive man with a slight edge in his voice that had her confused and worried?

Pete stepped behind the coffee bar and shrugged out of his coat. Thanksgiving was in a few days, and the cold was growing steadily deeper, along with the snow. "Good morning, Jan."

"Morning," Jan replied.

He stepped close. "Do you mind if we grab lunch today after church? I've got something I want to talk with you about."

Jan's mind raced and warring emotions played with her heart. Excitement at the chance to spend more time with Pete. Anxiety about what he wanted to discuss. But his face was peaceful, his eyes light. It didn't *seem* like he was asking her to lunch to call things off again.

She had said she would trust him. "I'd like that."

Pete's smile broadened. "Great. I'll meet you back here after classes." During the second service, they both usually attended one of several Bible study classes offered on Sunday mornings.

During their time at the coffee bar, Pete seemed more like his usual self. He joked with friends, teased

Landon with a donut, and winked at her from across the room. When he reached for her hand during service, Jan felt his grip on her heart tighten. It was a simple thing—someone to sit with during church or to hear his strong baritone singing the worship songs.

The last song after the message was about fighting battles on their knees. When Pete took a seat and hung his head in his hands, her heart cracked. Pete was in the middle of a battle, wasn't he? Unsure of what to do, Jan sat too and placed her hand on his back. She whispered prayers fervently over him for strength and wisdom and that Pete would be surrounded by God's spirit and supernatural deliverance from whatever was going on.

The song ended and the lights came up, but they sat there for a long minute before Pete lifted his head. "Thanks," he said softly.

"I'm here for you, Peter. Will you let me in?"

Pete nodded and squeezed her hand. "Lunch, okay?"

Jan leaned in and kissed his cheek before gathering her things. "I'll see you after class."

She wouldn't stop praying until then.

11

La Cresta proudly proclaimed they had "the best tacos in the Rockies." Pete usually agreed, but his appetite was nowhere to be found today. Church this morning had been everything he needed—a pointed reminder to fight his battles on his knees, not just with his weapons.

But in this case, he had prayed enough to be confident God wasn't expecting him to sit idly by. Which was a relief, because Pete wasn't sure he would have been able to obey that particular command. He slid into the booth across from Jan and nodded his thanks to the servers that dropped off chips and salsa before disappearing.

"How was your class?" He knew the question was lame, and that was confirmed by the way Jan raised her eyebrows at him.

"Is that what you're leading with? Come on, Pete. You don't have to make small talk with me."

She was right, of course. It was habit—put the mark at ease before you move the conversation toward the objective. But Jan wasn't a mark.

"Let's order first, so we don't get interrupted."

After they'd gotten drinks and placed their orders, Pete took a deep breath. "Okay. Here's the deal: there is a situation. A threat toward me—and you by extension."

The confusion was written all over Jan's face. "What? Why is someone threatening you? You need to go to the police."

Pete shook his head. "Heath is involved, and we are taking care of it. But Jan—" he grabbed her hand across the table, "—I really need you to stay somewhere safe for a few days."

She shook her head. "What? No. I mean, I'm not leaving. This is my home. And besides, where would I go?"

"I have a place for you and Aiden's family to stay." He kept his eyes on her, trying with every cell in his body to convey how serious the situation was.

"Are they in trouble, too? I have to call Aiden. They're on their way to Joanna's parents early tomorrow morning. If they need to cancel—"

"Breathe, Jan. If they are headed out of town

anyway, that works great. It'll be easier if I just have to worry about you, anyway."

He leaned back so the server could set down their plates. When she was gone, he leaned back in. "I know this is crazy. But I wouldn't ask you to leave if it wasn't serious. I just need to know you are safe while I take care of things."

Jan stared at a spot on the table, deep in thought. When she looked at him, he could see the uncertainty.

He reached for her hand again, tracing her fingers with his. Her deep, amber eyes drew him in, as though he could see his future there. As long as he could protect her. "I can't lose you, Janet. Do you trust me?"

JAN'S HEAD WAS SPINNING. There were so many unanswered questions. Who on earth would be trying to hurt Pete? Why hadn't he told her sooner?

What did this have to do with her?

Pete's question hung in the air. Did she trust him? Enough to up and leave town with no questions asked? It was crazy.

She'd been praying nonstop since she left him in the worship center, even skipping her class and settling in the prayer room at church instead. "Why do you have to be the one to take care of this, Pete? I don't understand. Why aren't the police involved?"

Pete's eyes dimmed. "There are some things I can't tell you at this point. Trust me, I wish I could. But I'm begging you to believe me when I say you need to leave town and let me take care of it."

Jan caught her lip between her teeth. "How long?"

The relief was palpable in Pete's response. "Just a few days. Maybe a week."

Jan nodded. "I'll have Courtney run the shop, but you have to explain this to Aiden." She pointed her finger at him to emphasize.

Pete held up his hands in surrender. "Absolutely."

Aiden was likely to demand he get involved once he heard. "You might want to wait until after he and Jo leave, so he can't interfere."

A smile played at the edges of his lips. "I think I'll take that advice. I don't blame him for being protective, though. He's lucky to have you. I'm lucky to have you."

Jan flushed with pleasure at the compliment. She could do this. Some random weirdo was apparently after Pete. This was a complete fluke. It's not like he had done anything to put himself in danger. Not like James and the whole running into burning buildings thing.

Jan squeezed his hand. "Whatever is going on, it's going to be okay. We can fight this battle."

Pete's wide eyes betrayed his thoughts, and his voice was slightly panicky when he replied, "You're going to be safe, hidden away—not fighting."

"Oh, I'll be fighting, too. On my knees." She wasn't going to leave him defenseless. And prayer was the best weapon anyone had.

Pete's shoulders dropped and he smiled. "You're amazing. That's exactly what I need you to do. How did I get so lucky?"

12

Pete drove up the mountain with Jan in the passenger seat. After she'd gotten things lined up for Courtney to run Stories and Scones while she was gone, Jan had met him at his office. Pete wasn't taking any chances, and he swapped his truck with Derek's Jeep. Derek owned a dog-training company based here in Freedom. It wasn't your typical obedience training for Fido the family pet, either. Derek trained search and rescue dogs, bomb-sniffing dogs, and drug detection dogs, among other things.

If there was any chance Knight had a tracker on Pete's truck, he didn't want the data to show that he'd been on the mountain. As they approached the cabin on the windy gravel drive, Pete's phone chimed with the motion sensor alert focused on the driveway.

He watched Jan's face as the cabin came into view, but it betrayed nothing of her thoughts. The cabin wasn't anything fancy, but it had its charms. The rustic log exterior and a front porch perfect for sitting with two wooden chairs waiting to oblige.

"This will be your home away from home," Pete said.

"Honestly, I thought I would be farther away. You made it seem like I would be going *away*. What are we? Twenty minutes from town?"

"Give or take. This is the perfect place. Close enough that no one would suspect it. And as far as property records, this cabin doesn't exist. No one will find you here."

They walked inside and stomped the snow off their boots. Pete disarmed the security system while Jan wandered inside. She pointed at the control unit after he made the beeping stop. "That's a pretty fancy system for a place in the woods."

Pete shrugged. "It's a safehouse."

"I guess we're lucky Heath has something like this available. What would normal people like you and I do in this type of situation without someone with his skills?" Her nervous laughter sounded forced.

He choked at her words. Of course she would

assume this was Heath's safe house. Got Your Six did have a few places, but none as secure as Pete's. What would Jan do if she knew that Pete had just as many skills as Heath when it came to things like this? She'd called him normal. That was all he strived to be since he retired.

Pete cleared his throat. "Yes, well, I'm just glad you're here and safe."

"What do we do now?"

"I'm going to start up the furnace and light a fire." He met her eyes. "Then I'm going to call Aiden. Why don't you check out the bedroom upstairs and the kitchen. If you make a list of supplies you need, I'll make sure you get them." Hopefully, that would give her something to do while he was on the phone.

He pulled the prepaid cell phone he'd picked up at Walmart out of his pocket. He'd already programmed Aiden's number in it. When Aiden answered, his voice was questioning. Probably due to the unfamiliar number.

"Hello?"

"Hey, Aiden, this is Pete O'Rourke."

"Pete? Did you get a new number?"

"Uh, yeah. Listen, I heard you and Joanna are out of town for a few days. There's something I need to talk to you about."

"Is this about you and my mom? You know I think it's great, right? You two are great together!"

Pete loved that Aiden was on board with the dating. And hated that he had to throw a damper on the whole mood. "Actually, that's not why I'm calling. We've got a situation here."

Pete explained, with a fair amount of vagueness, that he was keeping Jan at a safe house for a few days due to a threat toward Pete.

"I'm coming back," Aiden responded firmly

Pete was proud of the man's devotion to his mother, but he really needed him to stay away. "You're a good man and a good son. But the best place for you and your family to be is far away from here. Go have your Thanksgiving, and we will keep you up-to-date."

Aiden didn't respond for a long time. Finally, he said, "I don't like this, Pete."

"Trust me, I don't like it either. But I'm going to do absolutely everything in my power to keep your mom safe. Between Heath's team and myself, nothing is going to happen."

Another pause. Pete looked up at the ceiling with an unspoken prayer. Aiden sighed. "Okay. But I want updates, okay?"

"You got it."

"Can I talk to my mom?"

Pete handed the phone to Jan and stepped away to give them some privacy. He built a small fire before heading to the kitchen. The cabin was fully stocked; he'd been here less than a month ago and double checked his entire inventory. Still, he opened cabinets and evaluated their contents. When he had stocked his supplies, it hadn't been with anyone but himself in mind.

He would be fine with Vienna sausages and canned beans. But the offerings seemed pitiful now that Jan would be staying here. Not exactly five-star dining. Pete wanted nothing more than to give her all the best things—fun trips and fancy dinners. Instead, he was forcing her into a remote cabin alone for a week with canned tuna and crackers.

He pressed his hands into the counter and hung his head. Pete hated everything about this situation. Most of all, he hated that this was all his fault. He tensed slightly then relaxed as Jan's arms snaked around his hips. She hugged him tightly, her head resting between his shoulder blades.

Turning to face her, Pete wrapped his arms around Jan in return and looked down at her. There was no bright smile there to greet him, no mischievous twinkle in her eyes. Instead, there was a solemn acceptance and a hint of worry.

"I'm sorry about this," he whispered.

"It's not your fault," Jan replied.

If only that were true. He didn't argue though. Pete simply tightened his hold on her and dipped his head. The journey to her lips left ample opportunity for detours. He dropped a kiss on her forehead, her temple, and her cheek. Finally, his lips brushed hers. Hesitant at first, then searching. When Jan pressed up into the kiss, Pete hummed with satisfaction.

It was easy to imagine a life with Jan, waking up to her kiss each morning. Holding her close each night. Her vibrancy and her spirit brought color into his world. He traced his fingers down the length of her neck. She arched into his touch and his blood raced in response. He tempered his passion and softened their kiss.

He rested his forehead on hers and caught his breath. "Jan…" he breathed her name. The rest of the thought was lost. There was nothing but her.

"It's okay, Pete. I know."

He took a deep breath, memorizing the way she smelled, the way she felt in his arms. In all the years of running jobs in foreign countries, he'd never had so much on the line before.

His phone beeped with the motion sensor trigger on the driveway. It was Heath and Alexis, one of his team members. Heath had tasked her with guard duty at the cabin. Even though there shouldn't be anything to worry about here, it would be a load off Pete's mind to know Jan wasn't alone.

"I've got to go back into town and get things moving. You have my new number right?"

She nodded.

"Alexis is going to stay here with you. She'll be in contact with Heath and the team. If you need anything, let us know." He leaned down and kissed her again. "I'll be back before we leave town, okay?"

"Pete, are you sure you have to do this? Why don't you let Heath and his team handle it?"

No doubt it seemed strange to her, the insurance agent gallivanting off to confront a threat. "I wish I could. But this… It's personal. And he won't back down unless I'm there to make him."

JAN PAID little attention as Heath introduced her to Alexis. She seemed nice enough, perhaps a little intimidating with her black clothes and the gun strapped to her shoulder.

"Hi, Jan. It's nice to meet you." Alexis shook her hand and smiled. With her angular face and straight black hair, it seemed like she would fit better on one of those modeling reality shows Courtney was always talking about at the shop.

"Nice to meet you, Alexis."

"Call me Alex, please. No one calls me Alexis but my mother."

Jan grinned. "Well, I'm old enough to be your mom. Does that count?"

Pete shook Alex's hand. "Thanks for coming up

here. It will be nice for Jan to have someone to talk to."

"Happy to come. Heath told me how important it was. And besides, I didn't have any plans for the holiday anyway."

Jan frowned. A young woman like that should have a family to spend Thanksgiving with.

"Yes, well. We appreciate it." Pete turned to Heath. "Before we call him, I'm going to call Victoria. Mind if I do that now?"

Heath nodded. "Whatever you need. I'll just show Alex around."

Pete stepped into the kitchen, and Jan tried not to eavesdrop. Well, she didn't try too hard. Who was Victoria and why did Pete need to call her?

"Hey V. Yeah, I'm okay. I appreciate the heads up you gave me, but I wonder if you've got more info."

In the quiet cabin, Jan could hear the British accent through the phone, though some of the exact words were muffled.

"Oh really? That's great news. If that turns out to be true, it'll make this a lot easier. Any idea who hired him?"

Jan watched the easy smile Pete gave at the words of the mystery woman on the phone. Another twinge of jealousy made Jan shift in her seat.

"No, no. I think we will be okay. I appreciate the offer. I didn't think you'd still be in Denver. It's been almost a month since I saw you." He paused. "Just like that time in Kiev, huh? Well, I'm glad I'm not the only thing keeping you here. Just a bonus, I'm sure."

Was Pete flirting? Who was this woman? And more importantly, who was this man in front of her? Why was there a threat against him, and what sort of trouble was he involved in?

She couldn't help but wonder if she really knew Pete O'Rourke at all. She certainly didn't have the history with him that this Victoria did.

Finally, Pete ended the call and made his way back to the living room as Alex and Heath came from upstairs. Pete gestured to the door and looked at Heath. "I'm going to run back to town. Meet you at your office to make the call?"

Jan struggled to follow the conversation. Who were they calling?

Heath nodded, and Pete took two steps to cross the living room. He reached for her hand and squeezed it. "I'll be back tonight. Tomorrow morning at the latest." Pete leaned close to her ear, and Jan nearly trembled at the brush of his breath on her neck. "I'd kiss you right now, but I'd rather not have an audience when we do that again."

Heat washed from her ears to her toes as she recalled their kiss from only moments ago.

"I understand," she whispered back. She wrapped him in a hug. "Be safe."

He glanced back at her one last time before he walked out the door.

Heath showed Alex around the cabin, but Jan just stared at the closed door. Pete said he was coming back tonight or tomorrow, but the anxiety in her chest had risen with her arrival here. It was all a little too real now that she was ensconced at the safe house of a highly capable security firm, guarded by a gun-toting young woman who looked like she could probably take Aiden in a fight if needed.

Any illusion that this was just a bad dream or that it was really no big deal was shattered. She was spending Thanksgiving alone in a secluded cabin so a crazy person didn't take her out because of some grudge with her…boyfriend? She coughed a slight laugh at the word. Did women pushing sixty years old have boyfriends?

Jan sighed. Heath and Alexis were standing at the security panel looking at the screen. "I'm just going to go rest upstairs for a bit. It's been a long morning."

They waved her on, and Jan climbed the wooden stairs to the open-air loft. It housed a queen-sized bed, a small bookshelf, and a side table with a lamp. Jan traced her fingers over the quilt on the bed, then moved to examine the recessed bookshelf. The books were a seemingly random mix of genres and authors that would tell you nothing about the owner, except perhaps that they shopped for books at the local donation thrift store.

There were interesting knick-knacks though. Jan picked up a small lion figurine. It was heavier than expected, and she set it back down. She grabbed an Eiffel Tower candlestick from an upper shelf and tried to pull it down, but it didn't budge. What in the world? She tried again, and the top of the candlestick tilted forward. She heard the unmistakable sound of something mechanical behind the bookshelf.

Her fingers found the edge of the bookcase where it met the wall. Was that a gap? There's no way this was a secret room, right? She pushed on the shelf and it gave way into a black space. Jan stood at the entrance in shock and debated whether to explore further.

Unable to resist, Jan pulled out her cellphone and flipped on the light. She could see that the room was small. It might have been the closet originally designed for this loft. But why turn it into a secret room?

Jan ducked her head inside and saw the reflection of her cell phone light on a small black screen mounted on the wall just before the overhead light flipped on. She gasped and whipped her head back to the room. There was nothing there. Motion sensors?

The screen on the wall was illuminated too, and a floorplan of the house was displayed. It showed alarm status, motion sensors, heat signatures, everything. A button caught her eye: Main Floor Audio. She pressed it and jumped at the sound of Heath's voice.

"...here with Jan. I've got my phone and I'll be with Pete the entire..." Jan pressed the button again. Eavesdropping was not something on her to-do list. The other buttons were more concerning. Perimeter Armed. Vault Secure.

There was a vault? Heath and his team weren't messing around. She turned from the screen and noticed a handle on the back wall. She pushed gently, and the wall swung open to reveal a narrow staircase leading down.

This was too crazy. A secret command center with a hidden exit? What was this house used for? Jan shivered in the cold draft from the hidden stairway. She shut the door and backed out of the converted closet.

Jan moved the bookshelf back into place and tipped the Eiffel Tower back up. Then she slipped off her shoes and climbed onto the bed. There was nothing she wanted more than to fall asleep, but Jan laid on her back and stared at the ceiling for a long time before the weariness finally overcame her.

She was grateful to be here and be safe, but she

was especially grateful that this wasn't her life, or Pete's. Heath and his team were brave for protecting people the way they did, but Jan just wanted to return to her normal boring life. And she wanted that for Pete, too. The stress of this situation had to be getting to him. He wasn't experienced in these high-stakes situations.

13

Pete stepped inside the conference room at Got Your Six headquarters. He wasn't sure exactly what he expected from the private security firm offices, but this wasn't it. Cushioned leather chairs surrounded a giant rustic table sitting on an oriental rug. It felt more like the dining room of a large home than a conference room. On one wall, there were cabinets and a countertop with water bottles and other drinks.

Heath was already seated at the table, and Adam sat down across from him, gesturing for Pete to take a seat as well. "I think we found your boy Knight," Heath said. He clicked a remote in his hand and a huge black screen lowered from the ceiling. When it turned on, Ian's photo showed up. His face was partially obscured with a hat. "That's him."

"He's staying at the Lodge. Makes sense. It'd be easy to blend in with the other tourists there."

Heath was right. Freedom Ridge Resort was busy this time of year, and no one would think anything of another unfamiliar face coming and going.

Heath continued, "I called in a few favors. I might not work there anymore, but I still have a little pull." He clicked the remote again and an array of images showed up. "He's driving a dark-blue Ford Escape. We've got his room number and the fake name he's using. Strange thing, though. He checked out this morning."

Pete narrowed his eyes. Knight on the move wasn't likely to be a good thing.

"Pete, this is your rodeo. What's your plan?"

"We just need to draw him out. Ian Knight is wanted in at least a dozen countries, including this one. If I can convince him to meet and take him down, we can turn him over to the FBI. He's not going to go easy though."

Pete laid out the plan, while Heath and Adam jotted down notes. When he was done, Heath pressed down on a piece of wood in the center of the table, revealing a recessed compartment holding a conference phone and other electronics.

"Let's make the call. But first, let's pray."

It was one more reminder that Pete had chosen the right man for the job. They prayed and then Pete pushed the call button. The dial tone buzzed from the small speaker. "Is this line secure?"

"Untraceable," Adam confirmed.

He dialed the number and braced himself to hear Ian's voice.

"Is this O'Rourke?" Pete jerked back in surprise. The heavily accented Italian voice was definitely not Ian Knight's.

"Who is this? Where is Knight?"

"I thought it better we work directly from now on. I hired Knight to find you—and he did." So Victoria had been right. Ian was only the hired gun.

"Who is this?"

The man clucked his tongue. "I'm disappointed you don't remember me. After all, the night your people killed my brother, you shot me in the leg."

Pete's eyes widened. The name came out in a whisper. "Niccolo?"

"Ah, so you do remember me."

"I thought I killed you, Nico." As a matter of fact, the guilt from that particular encounter had been following Pete for more than fifteen years.

"You almost did. But it turns out I am stronger than my older brother. And it's been up to me to take over the business he left behind. Now, I just need Ariana." Nico laughed. "Well, her money anyway."

"This is crazy, Nico."

"Bring me the girl!" Niccolo's outburst gave away more than he intended. Pete met Heath's gaze across the table. Angry men made mistakes. They could use that.

"First, I want your guarantee that you won't hurt her." It was all part of his plan. Pete had to act like he was really going to deliver the girl, and that meant getting assurances she wouldn't be hurt. Ian would suspect something was up if Pete was too cooperative.

"She's my own flesh and blood. What kind of monster do you think I am?"

"I don't think you want me to answer that." Antonio might have been the brains of the operation, but Nico was the muscle. Pete had read the reports, and he didn't want to be anywhere near Nico when he got angry.

"You wound me, O'Rourke. But as long as Ariana gives me the accounts, I'll be out of your hair."

"I brought her to the States when she was twelve, with the expectation that I would never see her again. But…" he trailed off, waiting for Nico to take the bait.

"But what?"

Pete sighed, as though he was rethinking his willingness to share the information. "But she has instructions to follow if she received a call from me. A code word and a meeting place. And I have the same from her." All of this was a complete lie. Everything was put in place specifically so he would never see Ariana again.

"Where is the meeting place?" The eagerness in Nico's voice was unmistakable.

"She was adopted by a family that moved around a lot. US military. We chose a meeting place that was central within the US. It's in Omaha, at the airport."

The smile was almost audible in Nico's reply. "Call her."

"Nico, I can't…"

"Call her!" he barked.

"Fine. Once she hears the code word, she is supposed to show up within forty-eight hours."

"Excellent. Call her now, while I can hear."

Heath sent a text message to Alex, and they muted Nico's line, while they dialed in Alexis after she confirmed her role.

"Ariana?"

"I'm sorry, I think you have the wrong number."

"Ariana, I'm sorry. Firefly."

There was a long pause. Nice touch. "David, is that you?" Alexis put on a pretty convincing faded Italian accent.

"Firefly, Ari. Do you remember?"

"Yes, of course. I'll be there."

When the line went dead, Pete let out a sigh of relief. This was an unexpected twist. He had wondered who hired Ian, but he'd expected to have to face Knight at the fake meetup. It turning out to be Niccolo was a blessing.

From what Pete remembered, Nico hadn't been the sharpest cheese in the shop. Ian would have had contingency plans and exit strategies, but Nico would waltz in, overconfident and blinded by the prize.

He would no doubt be convinced by the fake call to Alexis, and they would take him down at the airport.

Now, Pete just had to go say goodbye to Jan and make the arrangements to get to Nebraska.

JAN HAD PACED the small length of the cabin a hundred times already and it was still the first day. Alexis stood unnervingly still, positioned in the corner opposite the door.

"Have you heard anything?" Jan asked her sole companion.

"Not since that call you heard."

Ah, yes. That call had made Jan very nervous, but she'd only heard part of it from the loft. Alexis spoke with some sort of fake accent. At first, Jan had some paranoid fear that Alex was working for the bad guy, but when Jan had asked, Alex had openly shared that she was pretending to be someone so they could lure the guy out.

At the time, it had all seemed very reasonable and Jan had simply accepted the answer. But now, being alone in the cabin was getting to her. She should be at Stories and Scones. This didn't involve her anyway. Wasn't Pete just being paranoid thinking she was at risk?

Some guy going through a rough time and threatening his insurance agent didn't seem like it warranted all of this. She walked around the safehouse again, stopping in the kitchen and opening the cabinets, just for the sake of having something to do.

When she opened the tall pantry cupboard, a set of hinges on the inside caught her eye. They weren't for the door, so why were they there? Her mind went back to the secret room upstairs. Would there be another one down here? Maybe this was the exit to those stairs.

With a glance at Alex, who was intently looking out the window and not paying attention to Jan at all, she pulled on the interior lip of the cabinet face. The entire shelf swung open.

A soft cry escaped Jan's lip when she came face to face with an entire arsenal of weapons. They hung neatly on hooks. From small pistols to large, scary looking guns, there had to be a dozen different weapons there. And were those grenades?

The stairway did, in fact, end inside the pantry, but the pantry was holding another secret. There was a doorknob on the bare wall. There was no window, but she placed one hand on the wall. It was cold to the touch, probably leading outside.

So, this cabin had a state-of-the-art security system, a secret exit, and a weapons cache that likely rivaled the entire arsenal of the Freedom Ridge Police Department. Exactly what kind of security work was Heath contracting?

"Whoa, what is this?"

Jan jolted at the sound of Alex's voice. Her hand flew to her heart, which was racing. "Oh my. Alex, you scared the living daylights out of me."

Alex gave an apologetic smile. "Sorry, Mrs. Clark. I wondered where you disappeared to. Looks like you found some of this cabin's dirty secrets."

Jan looked around the small room, trying not to look at the guns for too long. "I guess I did." Then Alex's words registered. "Wait... Didn't you know this was here?"

Alex shook her head. "No, Heath never mentioned it."

"I suppose it's reassuring to know he didn't think we'd need it."

"You're going to be just fine, Mrs. Clark. From what I heard, this operation will be a piece of cake."

"Yes, well, I'll be glad when this is all over.

Honestly, isn't Pete being a little ridiculous with all this? It's just one man with a little grudge."

A loud beep of the alarm ended their exchange, and Alex hurried over to check the display. "Front drive sensors. We've got company." One hand on her weapon, Alex checked her cell phone. Then she relaxed her stance and moved her hand. "It's just Pete. He texted a minute ago."

Jan closed the hidden pantry entrance and ran a hand through her hair. She'd been napping upstairs; her short hair probably resembled a cockatoo. Couldn't he have given her a little notice?

Too late now. She heard the slam of the car door, and moments later, Pete appeared at the front door. His smile was wide and Jan grinned in return, despite her irritation with being stranded at this cabin. He said a brief hello to Alex, then crossed the room to Jan.

She stepped into his arms and laid her head on his shoulder for a moment that ended too soon. Pete spoke first. "It's so good to see you."

"You too. Now, can I go home yet?" She raised her eyebrows, waiting for an answer.

Pete chuckled softly but shook his head. "Soon. I just came to say I'll be gone for about two days, but when I get back everything will be over."

"Two days? Pete, this is ridiculous. I'm going to go home. This doesn't even involve me!" Jan's frustration bubbled over. "I'm trying to trust you, but Pete—we can't live with a spirit of fear. Nothing is going to happen to me."

Pete's smile was gone and he squeezed her hands. "I need to show you something."

14

Jan stared at the photos on the coffee table in front of her. All ability to form coherent thoughts had suddenly fled. Her house. Her son. Their kiss? "I don't understand, Pete. Why would someone target me?"

Pete hung his head. "To get to me. Apparently, it is very obvious to everyone just how I feel about you."

Jan felt the inklings of pleasure at his words. The photo in front of her was pretty solid evidence that was true. "But why would someone target you?"

Pete didn't answer for a long time. Jan just watched the top of his head as he stared down at their linked hands. "The man who took these photos is someone I worked with a long time ago. He thinks by threatening you, I'll help him do something terrible. But I'm not going to."

Jan tried to reconcile his words with the actions of the last few days. "So this...coworker is going to break the law and what? He needs your help?"

"Pretty much."

"What could be so important that he is willing to threaten innocent people to get it?"

Pete shook his head. "People are greedy and broken, Jan. I wish I knew why he chose to do this. But all I can do is what I know is right. I'm going to stop him, and I'm going to protect you."

Fear washed over her. Seeing these photos and knowing that the man Pete was facing was perhaps more than just some disgruntled customer had her worried about whatever was about to happen. "But, Pete, you're just an insurance agent. Can't you just let Heath and his team handle this?"

"*Just* an insurance agent?" Pete's voice filled with mock horror. "I think you mean the best insurance agent in Colorado."

He smiled, but Jan couldn't return it. Jokes weren't going to make her worry go away. "Pete, be serious."

"Look," he said as he laid his hand on her knee, "I'll be totally safe. And Heath's team has my back. But I have to do this. No one threatens my family and gets away with it."

His family? Who was he talking about? Her confusion must have been evident, because Pete chuckled. "You're my family, Jan. And I'll do anything in my power to protect you from anything that threatens you."

He tugged gently on her hands, and Jan crossed the space between them to curl into his side. His lips brushed her hairline. "You're safe."

"I'll be fine here at Fort Knox. But what about you?"

"We've got this under control. Trust me?"

The subtle reminder of their previous conversations was not lost on Jan. "Trust you," she confirmed.

"You said you would do one other thing for me, too. Do you remember?"

Jan racked her brain. She remembered the trusting. Was there something else?

"You promised to pray for me, and I'd really love to do that together before I leave." He looked at her with hopeful eyes.

She swallowed and nodded. "Of course."

PETE TOOK one hand and wrapped the other around her waist, holding her to his side on the couch. She was tucked under his arm, and he'd never found two things that fit so perfectly together as the two of them.

He prayed quietly, just loud enough for Jan to hear. When he finished, Jan squeezed his hand.

"Father, keep Pete safe. And bring him home to me. Amen."

Pete murmured his agreement and then kissed her hair. "Thank you," he said.

He shifted his weight, but Jan protested. She pressed herself firmly into his side. "Just stay here for a minute longer."

"Whatever you need, Jan." It certainly was no hardship to hold her close and memorize her shape and scent.

They stayed motionless on the couch for a long moment, until Jan finally sat up and created some distance between them. "When you get back, we have a lot to talk about."

Pete nodded and gave a small smile. He knew he should walk away. Being in Jan's life had already put her in more danger than he wanted. But more than anything, he wanted to believe that this would never happen again and that he really could embrace a life with Jan.

Despite the depth of his feelings, he hadn't told her the truth. Not the truth about his former occupation, nor the truth about his feelings. He loved Janet Clark.

And once Nico Voltoro was out of the picture, he would be able to tell her. Both truths. She deserved to know about his past. But hopefully when it was well and truly in the past, it wouldn't be so overwhelming. He was afraid if she found out right now what was really behind all of this, Jan would run. That was the last thing he wanted.

For now, though, Pete had a job to do. And to do it right, he had to put aside all thoughts of Jan and any other distractions. And he had to become David O'Rourke, trained covert operative, and set aside Petey, hometown insurance agent. Just for a while.

He could do that. Pete leaned in and kissed Jan gently on the cheek, then touched his lips to hers. "Thanks for believing me. I know this is crazy, but knowing that you're safe is the only thing that I am worried about."

"Back at you," Jan replied.

Pete opened the door and waved to Alexis. "Take good care of her." Alexis gave a casual salute in response.

He took a steadying breath when he was back in the truck. It was show time.

15

The Omaha airport was small, but surprisingly crowded. Pete glanced around at the bustling terminal with confusion. Why was it so busy? The ticket he had purchased was purely to get him past security. All these other people were going somewhere.

He touched a small button on his watch, as though checking the time.

"Heath, any idea why the entire state of Nebraska is here?"

The response came quickly from Adam instead of Heath, his voice clear and crisp in the tiny earpiece Pete wore. "Tomorrow's Thanksgiving. It's the busiest travel day of the year."

"Of course it is," Pete grumbled to himself, not bothering with the button.

This could complicate things. If things got messy, it meant there was a lot of potential collateral damage. They'd just have to make sure it didn't get messy.

His phone rang, right on schedule based on the text they'd received. Pete picked it up but didn't say anything.

"I'm here. Where is she?"

"Relax, Nico. We meet inside the terminal. That's the deal."

"Maybe your deal. You get Ariana, you bring her to me."

"Nico, she's not just going to come with me."

"Then you make her, Mr. O'Rourke. Call me when you have the girl."

The line disconnected, and Pete talked to Heath again. "Did you get all that?"

"Loud and clear. Where do you think he is?"

"Not sure. Parking garage maybe? That's where I would be, but I would have eyes inside, too."

"Think he's as smart as you?"

Pete sure hoped not, but he was going to cover his bases. "I've got a plan but you need to be ready to move fast, okay?"

Out the window, Pete watched a plane land then taxi toward the concourse. Perfect.

He called Nico.

"She just landed. Where should we go?"

"I'll tell you when I know you are with her. We are watching. If my man doesn't see the girl, things will not go well for you or the nice people of Omaha."

His jaw tightened. Apparently, Nico was smarter than Pete gave him credit for. "Got it."

Pete stationed himself near the gate with the plane as it deboarded, watching the passengers flood out of the jet bridge.

Too old. Too blonde.

There. A young woman who could pass for around thirty. And her sweatshirt proudly displayed the Nebraska football logo. He fell into step beside her, as though he were a passenger himself.

"No place like Nebraska," he said conversationally, hoping she would take the bait.

She glanced his way with a friendly smile and he glanced at her sweatshirt. "Go big red! Are you going to the game Friday?"

That did the trick and the woman lit up. "I wish! I'm just home visiting my parents for the holiday."

"Oh, that's nice. I was planning to go, too. But my son is sick, so it looks like we have to cancel our plans." Pete hated the lying, but he knew he needed to walk through the main terminal in the company of a young woman, to keep this believable.

How far he would have to go was still to be determined.

"Oh, that's too bad." The young woman was drifting away, ending the conversation, but they were just passing the food court. He needed her to go farther. He knew that if he kept talking, she would likely be compelled to continue the conversation. Unless she felt threatened. But he had no plans to put her in any danger. He just needed that phone to ring.

"Yeah, my son is a huge fan. Just loves to watch them play. Do you have kids?"

"Nope," she responded, but offered nothing more.

Come on. Hadn't Nico's guy seen them yet?

"Oh, that's all right. You've got plenty of time. Or maybe you don't want kids. My wife tells me not to make assumptions, you know." Pete leaned in to the harmless old man character he was playing. "Our son is a teenager now, and—" His phone rang, interrupting his rambling.

"South garage, 2nd level. Gray suburban."

The line disconnected. Pete spoke to Heath. "Got it?"

"On it."

THE QUIET IN the cabin was starting to get to Jan. She was an extrovert in every way. The coffee shop was the perfect job for her, since she got to be surrounded by people all day. Sometimes, she thought that might be the only thing that helped her get through the quiet nights alone.

"Tell me about yourself, Alex. Are you new in town?"

"I moved here last year after Heath invited me to join Got Your Six. I met him while we were deployed."

"Marines, right?" There seemed to be no lack of former military around Freedom. Sometimes, Jan had trouble keeping track of which branch they served in, but she was pretty sure Heath had been in the Marines.

Alex nodded. "Yeah. I decided not to re-up after eight years in. Tired of being mostly surrounded by sweaty men who think they are God's gift to women."

Jan raised her eyebrows. There must be a story there, but she wouldn't push.

"So do you like working with Heath?"

Alex smiled. "Yeah, he's a great boss. I didn't know if I would find something I liked after getting out. But this seems like a good fit." Alex gestured around the cabin. "This is pretty sweet digs, isn't it?"

Jan nodded. "I suppose. It's a bit...fortress-y for me. But I suppose Got Your Six needs something like that every now and then."

"Yeah, it would be cool if we had a place like this. It practically defends itself."

Jan furrowed her brow. *If* they had a place like this? "What do you mean?"

"I mean, the security system is like nothing I've ever seen, and we've protected some pretty wealthy clientele. That weapons stash... All of it is military grade."

Jan shook her head. "No, what do you mean you wish Got Your Six had something like this. This belongs to Heath." Didn't it?

Alex frowned. "No. At least, I'm pretty sure it doesn't. Adam told me this cabin belonged to Pete. I guess he let Heath use it last year, but other than that, this is his secret safehouse. Pretty cool right? I guess this makes us part of the inner circle."

Jan's head was spinning. This cabin belonged to Pete? Which meant all the weapons belonged to him. And the security system. And the hidden exits.

Which all begged the question... Why did a small-town insurance agent need a safehouse anyway?

She'd known there was something Pete wasn't telling her about this whole situation. He kept so many of the details close to the vest about the man threatening them. But what else wasn't he telling her?

Jan was starting to think she didn't really know

Pete at all. Which was a bigger problem than she had hoped, since she'd foolishly laid her heart out on the line. She'd thought Pete was safe. Steady. But, judging by the threat on her life and the secret cabin with a weapons stash… Falling for Pete was far more dangerous than loving a man who fought fires and liked to skydive.

It was definitely dangerous for her life, as evidenced by being swept away to hide in this cabin. But worse, her heart was in danger of losing another man she loved. And she'd sworn not to do that again.

16

Pete stayed in communication with Adam and Heath as he made his way to the parking garage. The young woman was, thankfully, left behind at the baggage claim. Pete walked slowly, knowing that everything would come to a head. Nico's man had likely reported that Pete no longer had Ariana. They were taking a chance that the Omaha Airport police team would respond quickly to the reported threat in the parking garage.

Nico stood outside a black SUV and started yelling angrily when he saw Pete.

Sirens bounced off the concrete walls and blue flashing lights appeared out of nowhere as police cars drew closer.

Nico cursed in Italian and released a torrent of bullets in Pete's direction.

The impact registered first. Pete pressed a hand to his side, the warm, slick sensation confirming what he already knew. He'd been shot. The immediate lack of sensation was starting to give way to the hot, burning pain he was familiar with. It didn't feel serious, maybe a graze, but it was starting to sting like the dickens.

It was worth it though. Across the parking garage, airport security had descended on the car. Nico was spewing angry words in Italian as the officer placed the cuffs on him.

"No, this is a setup! O'Rourke! Where is the girl? You promised me the girl!"

Pete gave a small wave and ducked into the stairwell before the agents could make sense of the situation and detain him for questioning. He jogged down the stairs and found Heath and Adam in their mobile command unit.

Turned out, the TSA and local police were quite interested in the presence of an international criminal hanging out at the airport with a handful of stolen weapons. The weapons would make sure Nico didn't leave unless it was in the back of a squad car. The FBI and international warrants would make sure he didn't have the chance to bother Pete again for a very long time.

He slid open the van door. "Let's move."

Believing the Hero

"You're bleeding," Adam said from behind the wheel.

"And you're not driving."

Heath climbed into the backseat. "I'll take care of him. You just get us out of here before they lock down the garage."

Four hours later, the SUV was halfway across the state of Nebraska, sporting new license plates. Pete checked the bandage, but it looked like the bleeding had stopped. Another five hours or so and they'd be back in Freedom, and the entire situation would be behind him.

Then he could tell Jan exactly how he felt.

ALEXIS HUNG up the phone and looked at Jan. Jan bit her lip and waited for the update.

"They're on their way home. The guy is in custody and won't bother you again."

Jan sagged in relief. Praise the Lord!

"There was one thing," Alex said hesitantly.

Jan's smile fell.

"I guess Pete was shot. He's totally fine and they didn't seem concerned at all. But I thought you might want to know."

Tears filled her eyes as she processed. Pete had been shot? Different words echoed in her mind.

Words from a different night, ten years prior. *James had a heart attack. We couldn't get him out.*

She fumbled for the chair behind her and sank into it. This was like reliving the nightmare she'd had every night for almost a year after James had died. Would she have the same bad dreams now, but about Pete? Alex had said he was fine, but she couldn't shake the words. Pete was shot.

Despite her immense joy that he was okay and that the entire situation was over, there was another, stronger emotion pulling her under.

Fear.

She couldn't risk losing another man she loved. And protecting herself was going to mean cutting off whatever this relationship could have been with Pete. It was better that way.

"So they are on their way home?"

Alex nodded in response.

"Do you think we can leave then? I'd rather not stay here another hour I don't have to."

Alex looked around, glanced at her phone, and then shrugged. "Yeah, I don't see why not. I'll just text Heath and let them know. I think he said Pete could arm the security system from his phone."

Jan couldn't care less about the security system at that very moment. She just needed to be out of this cabin and away from all these reminders of Pete's lies. "Great," she forced the words to sound cheerful,

"I'll just go grab my things and meet you back down here."

Less than five minutes later, Jan slipped on her snow boots and followed Alex out of the cabin. Alex drove them down the mountain and dropped Jan off at her house. "Thanks so much for staying with me, Alex. I felt very...protected."

Alex smiled at her word choice. "My pleasure. I hope the rest of your holidays are much less exciting, but far more enjoyable."

Jan waved as Alex pulled out then shut the door behind her. Once inside, her smile fell and the small overnight bag hit the floor with a thud. Jan sat heavily on the bench in her entryway and hung her head in her hands.

17

Pete walked through the cabin, slowly since his side was still tender. He put things back in order and made mental notes about the supplies he would need to replenish. He had hoped Jan would still be here when he got back, but he supposed she had been eager to get home after being cooped up for four days.

If she was anything like him, Jan probably wanted to sleep in her own bed. It was late last night when they made it back from Nebraska and Pete had collapsed into bed. His text message to Jan had gone unanswered, but he was hoping it was simply because she was resting.

Of course, now it was mid-morning on Thanksgiving Day and she still hadn't replied. He pulled out his phone and sent another message.

PO: Happy Thanksgiving. I'm thankful for many things today, specifically that you are safe and that things can go back to normal. We need to talk soon. Can we meet up?

It wasn't until later in the day that his phone chimed with her response.

JC: I'm thankful you are safe as well. We do need to talk, but I'm tied up at the shop catching up and preparing for the Black Friday crowd this weekend. Can we talk Sunday?

Pete tried to read between the lines. Was there anything wrong? Texting was so frustrating. You couldn't read someone's meaning without hearing their voice or seeing their face. It was a reasonable excuse, though. No doubt Stories and Scones would be busy all weekend.

PO: That's fine. Can I take you to the Tree Lighting Ceremony?

JC: Aiden and Jo will be back, and I already promised Landon I would go with him. But I'll meet you there?

PO: It's a date.

Jan didn't respond, and Pete spent the next two days trying not to overanalyze her lack of enthusiasm. Sunday evening, Pete stood near the gazebo on town square, scanning the crowd for any sign of Jan or her family.

The Christmas Tree Lighting Ceremony was a

long-standing tradition in Freedom Ridge, and one of his favorites. The tree this year was huge, perhaps the tallest ever. Cheery Christmas carols played over the speakers as people milled about sipping hot chocolate and enjoying the event's signature peppermint bark treat. Children raced around the open space, chasing one another and squealing with laughter.

The sun was dropping rapidly, and by the time Mayor Starling was ready to hit the tree lights, the entire square would be illuminated by only streetlights and the twinkle lights hung on the gazebo. Pete's eyes searched the dim light and finally caught a glimpse of little Landon, riding happily on the shoulders of his father.

Pete's smile was automatic. Logically, he knew Jan's family wasn't his own. But maybe along with a beautiful woman, he would also be granted the opportunity to be Grandpa Pete. It had a nice ring to it.

He held up a hand and met Aiden's eyes as he walked towards them.

"Whoa! Landon, when did you get so tall? You must have eaten the entire turkey at Thanksgiving!" He filled his voice with exaggerated disbelief and was rewarded with giggles from the toddler.

"Hey, Pete. Good to see you," Aiden said.

"You too. Did you have a good trip?"

"We did. Especially after we heard everything was safe. Thanks for telling us."

Pete had texted Aiden as soon as his wound was bandaged. "Of course. I know it was probably hard for you to be so far away from your mom." Pete glanced around. "Speaking of which... Is she here?"

"Yeah, she's over with Jo." Pete's gaze followed Aiden's extended finger back toward the hot cocoa vendor.

"Thanks. I think I'll go over and meet them. I could use something warm, too." He rubbed his hands together and blew into them. "I forget how cold it gets when the sun disappears."

Aiden smiled. "Sounds good. Tell them we'll be checking out the tree and picking our ornament." The mayor's wife had a tradition of letting the children decorate the tree with ornaments each year. It was hilarious and heartwarming all at the same time.

Joanna saw Pete first, and pointed him out to Jan, who turned around while he was still a few steps away. Oh, it was good to see her face.

"Hey, Pete." Joanna's greeting disappeared as Pete pulled Jan into his arms. It was like the tension of the threat against her and the adrenaline of the sting hadn't fully faded until he saw her in person. As much as he knew she was safe four days ago, his heart hadn't processed it until this moment.

Jan was stiff in his arms for a moment, then

finally relaxed and she laid her head on his shoulder. "I missed you," he whispered in her ear. She lifted her head and he met her eyes. They held the tiny reflection of the white twinkle lights on the cocoa hut, but behind the manufactured ambience of the event, her eyes were shadowed and dull. "What's wrong?"

JAN RESPONDED with a small shake of her head. "In a few minutes, okay?" She needed more time. Which was crazy, because she'd had four days to prepare for this. Four days to ready her heart to shut the door on a relationship with Pete.

Apparently, it wasn't enough.

He nodded, but his smile had dimmed. While they waited for their names to be called for their drinks, Pete grabbed her hand. "How was Black Friday? I thought about stopping by, but I didn't want to fight the crowds."

"It was busy. I ran a special deal on books, so that brought in a lot of people. Between that and everyone's caffeine addiction, we did pretty well." It was the first year Jan had tried to capitalize on the Black Friday shopping trend, and the book sale had proven itself worthwhile. It was also the first year Jan found herself attempting a little retail therapy of her own by swinging by several shops on the Square. A few candles from Wick and Sarcasm, the local candle shop, found their way home with her.

Finally, the barista called their names and they went to find Aiden and Landon near the tree. Jan watched Aiden with Landon, so gentle and loving. It was almost painful the way it reminded her of how James had been with Aiden. She prayed every day that Aiden would get to see the fullness of Landon's life. Aiden was just as adventurous as his father, perhaps even more.

"Think we can sneak away to talk? There's still about fifteen minutes until the ceremony starts."

Jan nodded and followed Pete to a quiet spot behind the gazebo. Since the bench they sat on faced away from the tree, no one else was nearby.

Jan held her hot chocolate on her knees and stared at the lid. Pete's gaze was on her, and she sent a desperate prayer to God asking for the words she needed.

"What's going on, Jan?" His inquiry came softly, the sadness already lacing his words.

She swallowed and tilted her head to look at him. "I can't do this, Pete."

"I know the last week was a little crazy, but I wanted to talk to you about that."

"A little crazy? You got shot! And it's not just that.

I realized just how little I know about Peter O'Rourke."

"That's not true. You know me better than anyone. There is just something I couldn't tell you."

"Does it have anything to do with why you own a secret cabin in the woods with a security system that would make Freedom Community Bank jealous?"

He shifted his weight. "Umm, yeah, kind of."

"So what is it? Did little Petey O leave town and join the mob or something?" Jan raised her eyebrows to let him know she was waiting.

"Not exactly. You know how I worked for the USGS?" He waited for her nod. "Well…I didn't. I was a CIA operative for twenty-five years."

Jan blinked. "I'm sorry. I could have sworn you just said CIA operative. As in…a spy?"

Pete shrugged lightly. "We don't call ourselves that, but yeah. That's the basic idea."

Jan's mind raced, trying to reconcile the safe, slightly nerdy Pete O'Rourke she knew from high school and here in Freedom with some other version of him that, in her mind at least, was more like Jason Bourne. Had he really spent twenty-five years gallivanting around the world working for the CIA?

"I-I thought you reviewed flood maps?"

Pete's guilty, close-lipped smile was almost endearing. He looked up at her, since his head hung. "I'm sorry I lied. I couldn't exactly come home and tell everyone the truth. Who would believe me? And if they did, it was too dangerous." He waved his arms through the air, gesturing to her. "Obviously."

Jan shook her head in denial. "You could have told me. You could have told James."

"I tried once. He thought I was joking. But it became easier to ignore it. Not many people cared about my boring job for the government. And once I opened my insurance agency, no one needed to." He shifted on the bench and took her hand. The gloves she wore dulled the sensation of his grip, but she remembered enough to know how it would feel. "My biggest regret is that I didn't get to tell you before this all happened."

Jan sighed. "I appreciate you telling me now. But it doesn't change anything. I still can't do this," she said, echoing her earlier words.

"Why not?"

"It's too much. You've got an exciting, dangerous past that tells me you seek that adventure just like James did. And clearly, it's impossible for it to stay entirely in the past, which is why you have that cabin in the woods filled with more weapons than I've ever seen."

Pete's shoulders sagged. "Found that, did you?"

"Mmm-hmm. But it's all of it. It's the secrets. It's the danger. It's the fact that I'm not an exciting woman."

"I'm not looking for a thrill, Jan. I've been there, done that. For ten years, I've barely left Freedom Ridge. Can't you see I'm not Special Operative O'Rourke anymore? This mission—which I only did to protect you—proved that! I'm not young anymore. I used to live for the opportunity to take down a criminal, or turn an asset. But now? There is nothing I want more than a quiet life here—with you."

Jan felt her eyes water. His words were enticing. What woman wouldn't want to hear that? But it didn't matter what he wanted. Pete's past would always be there, threatening to come to the surface and put him—and her family—in danger.

"I'm sorry, Pete. I can't risk it. These people can't be the only ones who know how to find you. I can't handle losing someone else. And I won't put Landon or Aiden or Jo at risk either."

She straightened her head, her chin tilted up as she forced herself to look him in the eyes. There was hurt in them, but she saw the moment he accepted her stance. With a slight nod, he released her hands.

"I understand. I wish it could be different."

"I do, too."

18

From the gazebo, Pete watched as Jan returned to Aiden, Jo, and Landon. She knelt down beside the little boy, and he wrapped his arms around her neck. As much as he hated it, Jan was right. Hadn't he had the same argument with himself a hundred times about how selfish it was for him to try to have a relationship.

After ten years. He'd really thought he was in the clear, though. He'd even considered selling the safe house last year. It made much more sense for Heath to have it, and it had been basically unused the entire time Pete had lived in Freedom Ridge.

Until this week.

Jan was right. There was no way to guarantee his past wouldn't come back to haunt him again. The best thing he could do to protect the people he loved would be to stay unattached.

He was still the lone wolf he had always been, just now older and grayer. He watched as Mayor and Mrs. Starling kicked off the ceremony by introducing Daniel, the featured musician. The words of "Joy to the World" fell flat on his soul as families around him laughed and sang. It might be nearly Christmas, but Pete was feeling more like Scrooge than Santa.

Instead of staying, he stepped away as the song ended.

Addison and Ty waved at him, but he didn't bother responding as he trudged back toward his truck. Across the square, he turned back on his way just in time to see the lights turn on and the crowd cheer.

"Merry Christmas, Petey," he said to himself. It was going to be a long December.

PETE WAS DETERMINED NOT to let Jan's rejection ruin his daily routine, or their friendship. The surprise was evident on her face when he walked in the door of Stories and Scones on Monday morning.

"Oh! Good morning, Pete."

"Morning. Did you have a good time at the ceremony last night?"

Jan nodded. "Landon was so tired by the end, but yes. It was lovely."

"I'm glad. I'll just take a cappuccino, please."

Jan looked at him for a moment. He fought the urge to squirm. It was his usual drink, but somehow he felt awkward and out of place. Was this how it was going to be? Was Jan going to ask him to leave?

But she simply rang in the order and gave him his total then grabbed a scone and a cookie from the case. "Here, try my new flavors. Orange and cranberry spice for the scone. And one of the pumpkin snickerdoodles you liked so much."

He protested lightly, but Jan held out the small parchment bag. "Please take them." Pete met her eyes. It wasn't just a scone. It was a peace offering of sorts.

"Thanks. I'm sure it is delicious."

Every day that week, things became more normal. And with each friendly encounter, Pete's hopes that he might end up with Jan in the end grew a little dimmer. Jan acted perfectly cordial, but he missed her sharp wit and teasing jokes at his expense.

Preparing to meet with a family who had reserved the cabin on Scenic Road, Pete opened the safe in his office. His eyes fell on the black, unlabeled key for the safe house. For ten years, he had kept that house stocked and ready. For what? An attack? Had he always known his past would come to haunt him? Maybe so.

Or maybe, a part of him liked having that secret. To know he wasn't just a boring insurance agent. If he was being honest with himself, for ten years he had been just that. Until a month ago, when Victoria showed up and warned him, Pete had been living a boring, predictable life. And that was what he wanted to do. Jan might think he needed the excitement of the unknown and dangerous, but what he really needed was the excitement of being with her.

He shut the door to the safe when he heard the front door of the office open. He checked his watch. The Schumacher's weren't supposed to pick up their key for another few hours. Tessa's greeting could be heard through the wall.

"Hey, Aiden!"

What was Jan's son doing here? Was everything okay? Instead of waiting for Tessa to call him, Pete set the keys on the desk and opened his door. Aiden stood by the desk, chatting with Heath's sister.

"Aiden. Good to see you. What brings you by?"

Aiden glanced toward the back office. "Do you have a minute to talk?"

Pete extended his arm into the doorway, inviting Aiden into the small room.

Instead of taking his usual seat behind the desk, Pete sat in one of the chairs reserved for his clients and indicated that Aiden should take the other. "What's going on?"

Aiden leaned forward, his elbows resting on his knees and his hands steepled under his chin. "I don't want to butt in where I'm not welcome. I've got to know what happened between you and Mom—and she's not talking."

Pete sighed. "Aiden... If she doesn't want to talk to you about it, I'm not sure it's my place to tell you."

Aiden leaned back. "That's what I was afraid of. She's being so stubborn about this. I don't understand. The two of you seemed so good together. You made her really happy."

Pete listened, unable to disagree. "I thought so, too. But your mom... She knows what she wants, and it isn't me." The words tasted bitter as he spoke them. Jan had made it very clear that she didn't want Pete with all his baggage.

Aiden shook his head. "See, that's where I think you're wrong. Since the tree lighting, Mom hasn't been herself. She's quiet and grumpy, even short-tempered, and she is the most patient person I've ever met. I think she misses you."

"She's allowed to be grumpy, Aiden. It doesn't mean she regrets her decision."

"So it was her decision to end things?"

Pete pressed his lips together. Was he crossing the line of sharing too much? "Let's just say if it were up to me, we'd never spend another Christmas alone."

Aiden nodded. "That's what I figured. Thanks, Pete." He stood and Pete mirrored the action automatically.

"That's all?"

"Yeah. I needed to know if you still had feelings for her and that I was right to assume it was Mom who had called it quits."

Pete shook his head. "Look, Aiden. It's not that simple. There is a lot you don't know. What happened at Thanksgiving, it was my fault. It isn't fair to ask your mom to carry my burdens forever."

"Isn't that what love is all about?" Aiden laid a hand on Pete's shoulder. "We've all got baggage, Pete. We either struggle to carry our own every day, or we share the load with someone else, trading on and off when it becomes too much. My mom's got her own baggage. And I think it's the weight of that she's struggling with right now, more than she is scared of yours."

Aiden's words struck Pete and he stood silently as Aiden left the office. Shouldn't Pete be the one sharing his wisdom with the young man? Instead, Aiden had spoken with insight far beyond his years. He'd given Pete a lot to consider.

Perhaps Jan's retreat from their relationship did have more to do with her own history than it did with his. But how did that help? She'd still retreated, and he still couldn't do anything about it.

But the seed was planted. Just when Pete had closed the door on the idea of a future with Jan, Aiden had stopped by and opened it again. A glimmer of hope had taken root. Using that glimmer as fuel, Pete would pray once again for the woman he was sure was the only one for him.

When Tessa knocked on his office door a week later, he was staring aimlessly at the paperwork in front of him. He'd been doing that a lot lately, in fact. If he could somehow convince Jan to give him another shot, maybe it could all work out.

"Sorry to interrupt. I was just wondering what kind of candy you want me to get to throw out at the parade?"

Pete struggled to catch up. "Parade?"

"It's this Friday. I already registered, so all you have to do is show up Friday afternoon and get in line. But I know all the parade floats usually throw out candy, so I didn't want you to look stingy or anything."

Tessa's lighthearted rambling usually made him smile, but he was too stunned to reply.

She must have caught on to his surprise. "Or I could cancel your registration," she said tentatively.

Pete shook his head. "No, no, I should do it. You'll ride along with me?"

Tessa shrugged. "Sure. I can throw candy as well as anyone. Are you sure you don't want someone else to ride with you?"

He knew what she was asking. She'd seen his relationship with Jan grow during the month of November, and like everyone else in town, was apparently afraid to ask what had happened.

"Yeah. There's no one else. Not anymore."

Tessa's eyes filled with sympathy and Pete shrugged.

"It'll be okay, I promise. Just say you'll ride shotgun at the parade?"

"You got it, boss." She gave a cheeky salute along with the perky reply.

Pete smiled that time. "Good. I also have to get the lights up on the truck, I guess." Except for a few years ago, when a blizzard had shut down the town and canceled the parade, Pete's insurance company had sponsored a float. It was really just a classic

1960's pickup that he decked out with Christmas lights and a magnet with his company logo on it.

"Let me know if you need help with that," Tessa offered. "I tried to convince Heath that Got Your Six needed a float this year, but he wasn't going for it."

"Yeah, he mentioned that to me. Parade floats aren't generally high priority when you're protecting people."

Tessa sighed. "I know. I actually think Claire and I might have convinced Heath, but Adam was being a big ol' killjoy—as usual. He makes me crazy."

Pete raised an eyebrow at her tone. It was no secret that she and her brother's business partner didn't get along. Perhaps the reason Adam was under her skin went a little beyond just his being a stick in the mud.

"Maybe next year I'll let you get more creative with my float. I've used my dad's truck for the last five years at least."

Tessa smiled kindly. "I think the fact that you are participating at all is appreciated around here. Freedom doesn't expect everyone to be flashy. The community is just stronger when everyone is involved, you know?"

"Freedom is a pretty special place," he agreed. He would know. Pete had seen the world and settled on right here. Sometimes, he envied people like Tessa who had figured it out without the need to wander first.

Jan huddled next to Joanna on the sidewalk as the fire trucks rolled by, covered in white lights and playing Christmas music as the firefighters walked alongside and handed out candy. Landon squealed when he saw Aiden and ran up to him.

Aiden stopped and picked him up, letting him throw a handful of candy to some kids before bringing him back over to them. "Here you go, bud. You stay with Mommy and Gigi while I finish the parade. You don't want to miss seeing Santa!"

Mention of the man in the red suit squashed all of Landon's protests, and soon Aiden and the firetrucks were a block away. Jan's good mood evaporated when the familiar vintage red truck drew closer.

Only a few weeks ago, they'd discussed the possibility of Jan riding alongside Pete in the parade. Seeing her spot filled with someone, even someone as sweet as Tessa, made her wonder if she'd made the right decisions. Pete had one arm out the window, waving and occasionally tossing candies at the feet of the children on the curb.

Landon's little voice called out to him as he waved enthusiastically.

Pete smiled and threw a bunch of candy at her grandson. Her eyes never left him, but his gaze never met her own. She felt her eyes water and blinked away the tears.

Would it ever get easier to live here in this town with him if they couldn't be together?

19

Jan dutifully stacked blocks, counting them out loud one by one, until Landon gleefully knocked them over before putting his hands together asking for more. Aiden sat on the couch with a football game on the television across the room.

"Should I still plan on you for Christmas Eve service and dinner?"

Aiden nodded. "Of course. Anyone else coming this year?"

Jan smiled. She had a habit of adopting those in Freedom without a family. "I think Alexis is coming. Connor is coming and bringing Luke with him." She had a soft spot for the single father who worked at the fire department. "Maybe you could invite Tuck?"

"He might be spending the day with Patience, but

I'll check."

The volunteer firefighter was a friend of Aiden's and had just started working at Patience's bakery, and Jan had noticed the two of them getting pretty close lately.

"That makes sense. I hope it's true. Oh, I thought maybe Adam would want to come, too."

"That sounds great. Is Pete coming like usual?" Her son's attempt to keep his question casual was blatantly transparent.

"I haven't invited him," Jan admitted.

"Why not? Pete has been at our house for Christmas for at least the last three years, right?"

Jan stacked the blocks again before responding. "Not that it is any of your business, but Pete and I aren't going to be spending as much time together."

Aiden dropped all pretense of disinterest and leaned forward on his knees. "What happened, Mom? Before Thanksgiving, the two of you seemed closer than ever."

A twinge of pain squeezed in her chest. They had been closer than ever. Her lips nearly tingled at the memory of their brief kisses.

"Things change, Aiden. It's not going to work out for me and Pete. Maybe me and anyone." She didn't meet her son's eyes. Instead she focused on Landon and his sweet giggles. "Can you stack the blocks?"

"Help me understand, Mom. Dad's been gone a

long time. Don't you think—"

Jan cut him off. "This is not about your father." Immediately, she regretted her harsh tone and took a deep breath. "This is between Pete and myself."

A moment passed and Aiden nodded. "Fair enough. Can I just say one thing?" After she agreed, he continued. "I don't know everything that happened while you were tucked away at Pete's cabin. But I know that Pete did everything he could to keep you safe, because he loves you. I'm sure you are afraid, and believe me, I understand. When Joanna was kidnapped, it was the most terrifying experience of my entire life. The idea of something happening to her still keeps me up at night. But if it did? More than anything else, I would be grateful for the time God has given us. Giving up those moments out of fear of the future? Not only would I have missed out on everything amazing, but I would be making security an idol, instead of placing my trust in God."

As she listened to the wisdom of his words, Jan nearly cried. When had her son gotten so grown up? She still thought of him at six, with a broken wrist from rollerblading, or at fifteen learning to drive for the first time. Even twenty-two and back home from college with a confidence he could conquer the world and the naïveté to think it would be easy.

But sitting across from her now was a man.

Believing the Hero

It wasn't the first time she'd had the realization, but perhaps it was the most poignant. Even though he was an adult, she'd always been the one he came to for advice—and here he was giving it instead.

"Maybe you're right. It's a lot easier said than done, though."

Aiden stood up and gave her a hug. "I'll be praying for you, okay?"

"Thank you. That's exactly what I need." She tickled Landon's toes. "Well, that, and a few more hours with this guy!"

After Aiden and Landon left, Jan was left to face the quiet of her cozy cottage house once again. She didn't decorate as much for Christmas as she used to, but the tree was up—an artificial one these days instead of the live fir James had always cut down himself. There were four stockings on the mantle. Aiden, Joanna, Landon, and herself. On the mantle above, the collection of framed family photos had been pushed to one side to make room for a small Nativity scene.

She picked up one of the photos. It was James and her in front of Hidden Falls. "Oh, James, what am I supposed to do?"

Jan felt a touch silly. After he had died, she'd talked to him every day. It had been the only thing that kept her going. But she hadn't spoken to him out loud in years. Why did she feel the need today?

"You'd be so proud of our son. Did you hear him today? Telling his old mom she needs to put herself out there and not be afraid to take risks. Sounds like something you would have said." He'd always been a risk-taker.

"Is he right? Am I just being fearful and not trusting God?" Jan wanted to trust the Lord with her life. Her faith was deep enough to know there was nothing better than the plan God had for her. But her heart? She was scared.

"God? Help me trust you. I'm tired of being afraid. I don't want to miss out on the blessings You have because I think I can control things. Your Word says You have given us a spirit not of fear but of boldness and love. I'll be honest, I don't feel very bold these days. I need Your help."

Her fingers trailed the photo of her husband, but her thoughts drifted to Pete.

She'd been convinced that Pete was God's plan for her. Until fear caught up. She prayed for wisdom about that relationship. It had grown so confusing over the last month, but being with Pete felt so right. Could she let go and trust that God was in control? Could she take the risk that something might happen? Whether it was because of Pete's past or not, he wouldn't live forever. At least not here on Earth.

Neither would she.

But if she hadn't missed her chance, maybe they could live the rest of their 'not forever' together.

She just had to figure out how to tell Pete what she wanted.

WAS THERE anything more depressing than buying yourself a frozen turkey dinner to eat on Christmas Day? If there was, Pete couldn't think of it at the moment. He stood in front of the frozen section and contemplated his options.

He knew if people found out he had no plans, he could get invitations to half a dozen places for the holiday. But he didn't want to go to Heath and Claire's house, or even the Pembroke's. He wanted to go to Jan's house, like he had the last three years.

With a sigh, he opened the door and grabbed the TV dinner. Next year, he was going to the beach for Christmas. What did they serve at a Caribbean resort on Christmas?

The cashier was far too friendly, and the way her little Santa hat jingled grated on his nerves. "Merry Christmas!" Pete did his best not to earn a reputation as a grinch. He gave a tight smile as he paid for his groceries, then carried the bags to his truck, the packed snow of the unplowed parking lot crunching under his feet. Tomorrow was Christmas Eve, and

Pete knew his Christmas spirit was at an all-time low.

He laid his forehead on the steering wheel as he waited for the truck to warm up. "God," he whispered, "help me remember to be joyful in all circumstances. This is Christmas. No matter what else is going on in my life, this is a reminder of the best thing that ever happened to me. You sent Jesus into the world. And even though I am all wrapped up in my own misery, I don't want to be anymore. If I'm going to be alone, then help me be content with that."

When Pete pulled in to his house, he frowned at the dark porch. He hadn't put out any Christmas lights this year, being pretty Grinch-y and all. His house looked sad when compared to the neighbors' houses twinkling with lights.

When he stepped toward the front door in the dim light of the evening, he saw a shape huddled on one of the Adirondack chairs.

"Jan?" He looked back and finally realized her car was parked across the street. "What are you doing out here? It's freezing!"

He ushered her inside, convinced he was going to have to call Aiden and explain why his mother had frozen to death on Pete's front step.

"I'm fine, Pete. I just needed to talk with you."

He scowled at her and fixed a cup of cocoa. "Well,

you could have waited in the car. Or come inside. You know very well where the spare key is hidden." He grabbed another blanket from the couch and threw it over her legs while the water heated up in the microwave.

Jan rolled her eyes, but he still thought she looked pale. "I'm fine. Please stop."

Pete stopped moving for the first time since he'd seen her on the porch. The lack of activity meant there was nothing to distract him from the fact that Jan was here, feet away from him. She was close enough to touch, and every part of him was aching to do so.

"Why are you here?" He hadn't intended it to be, but his tone was accusatory, the hurt seeping through despite his best efforts.

The microwave beeped that the water was done. He turned to remove it, but Jan held up a hand.

"Wait. Don't worry about the water. I just have something to say, and then I'll be on my way."

What did that mean? Was it bad, and that is why she wasn't staying? Pete forced himself to stay still and watch her face.

Jan wrung her hands, and Pete resisted the temptation to take them between his own.

"Aiden says I'm living my life in fear and missing out on God's best by not trusting Him."

Pete bit the inside of his cheek to keep from

revealing just how glad he was that Aiden had stuck his nose in their business. Instead, he lifted his eyebrows. "Oh?"

Jan nodded. "I'm afraid he's right, Pete."

The vulnerability of her admission nearly broke his resolve to keep his distance. She continued before his internal struggle was lost.

"Losing James was the hardest thing I've ever experienced. The idea that something could happen to you if we were together just… I don't think I could go through it again."

"Nothing is going to—" Pete stopped himself. He knew that was an empty promise. No one knew what would happen tomorrow except the Lord. "Janet, I can't promise that something won't happen to me. Just like you can't promise nothing will happen to you—which, by the way, would absolutely wreck me, too."

"I know we can't. And I know that I should trust that God is in control. My worrying about it won't change anything, and if my fear means missing out on a life with you… Well, I don't want to be afraid anymore."

Pete's heart leapt at her words. A life together. He stepped close and wrapped his arms around her. After a moment with her head tucked against his shoulder, he pulled away to meet her eyes.

"If I'm granted a life with you, I promise not to

take unnecessary risks. And I promise to make sure we both live every day with no regrets."

"I promise to be honest with you about my fear, and to lay it down at the Lord's feet when it happens. I won't pull back from you."

"Oh, love. We'll take it to God together, okay?"

Then, he lowered his lips to hers and sealed the promises. The kiss was sweet and deep, and he lost himself in the rightness of being together again. It was the missing piece from the last month falling neatly back into place. But this time there were no loose edges or missing gaps. They were both going in with eyes open, knowing the risks but moving forward anyway. Pete cupped his hand along the nape of her neck, her short hair soft under his skin. He breathed her name, filled with more promises—unspoken ones this time. He kissed her again, one last gentle caress before his lips pressed against her forehead and he held her close to his chest.

"I wouldn't have blamed you for not wanting to take the risk. My past is…complicated."

"So is mine," she replied. "But love is worth the risk, isn't it?"

Love? He smiled and kissed the crown of her head. "Yes. You definitely are."

20

"You were going to eat a TV dinner for Christmas?" Jan couldn't keep the horror out of her voice as everyone took their chairs around the table.

Alexis laughed quietly. "That's pretty bad, man."

Pete blushed. "Well, it was either that or a peanut butter sandwich."

Jan scoffed. "Such a man. You'd think after forty years as a bachelor, you would have learned how to cook."

"Thankfully, a beautiful woman takes pity on me every now and then." Pete winked at her, and Jan felt heat rise in her cheeks.

"What's a TV dinner?" The words of Connor's son, Luke, made everyone laugh.

"You're better off not knowing, kid," Pete said with a chuckle.

Connor gave an embarrassed shrug. "Oh, he has definitely had one. It's not like I do much cooking."

Jan patted his shoulder. The single dad had lived in Freedom for less than a year, and Aiden had promptly taken the younger firefighter under his wing. Which meant she had as well.

"I'm glad you're here, then. I love to cook for people who will appreciate it."

"I've never met someone who doesn't appreciate your cooking, Janet." Pete's casual compliment thrilled her all the way down to her toes.

"He's right, Mom. You spoiled me for anyone else's cooking." Aiden's eyes widened, and he looked toward his wife with a sheepish smile. "Other than Joanna's, of course."

The table laughed when Jo rolled her eyes. "Nice save."

Jan set a basket of warmed rolls in the center of the table and clapped her hands together in satisfaction. The spread was simple but just as abundant as the love that surrounded the table.

"That's everything. I'm so glad you are all here." She debated for a moment, looking at her son before turning to Pete next to her. "Pete, would you say a blessing?"

"I'd be honored." Pete grabbed her hand, and everyone around the table mirrored the motion, joining the mismatched collection of people in a circle. To her, it seemed the perfect representation of what Christ had done for people, as well. The family of Christ was filled with people from every walk of life, every color, and with every kind of redemption story.

After dinner, Aiden grabbed the remote and turned the music up. Jan couldn't help the smile that spread across her face. Dancing after Christmas Eve dinner had been something James always instigated, and Aiden had continued the tradition after his father died. Admittedly, she had cried through the dance for the first few years, but now, she simply enjoyed the laughter and joy that came along with "Rocking around the Christmas tree" with her son.

As the music played, Landon bounced up and down, bending his knees in a semblance of a dance that more closely resembled an Oompa Loompa and made Jan laugh out loud. Alexis pulled Luke into dancing, though he didn't disguise his lack of enthusiasm. Probably too cool at this age.

"Merry Christmas, Mom."

Jan gave a happy sigh. "Merry Christmas, sweetie."

She felt Aiden gently leading her across the room and she gave him a puzzled look.

Then Aiden released her waist and stepped back.

He looked over her shoulder. "I think it's about time you cut in."

Jan felt herself freeze. Pete's voice was quiet. "Are you sure?"

Aiden nodded. "I'm always happy to dance with my mother, but I also know when it's time to step aside and make room for another man in her life. I couldn't be happier that it is you, Pete."

Aiden shook Pete's hand, and Jan couldn't help the tears that escaped. Pete stepped in front of her and took her hand. He ducked his head and she met his gaze. "Hey. Don't cry. I don't have to…"

Jan shook her head. Pete knew the origins of this tradition. He'd watched her dance with James and then Aiden for years. "I want you to," she choked out.

She looked at Aiden. "Thank you, Aiden." It couldn't be easy for him to see another man step into the spot that used to be his father's, but once again, Aiden was proving to her that he had grown up to be a mature, godly man. Pride swelled within her. Soon, it was replaced by the sweet peace of dancing slowly with Pete in her small living room.

"Bye! Thanks for coming!" Jan waved goodbye to Connor as he walked away from the house, his son trailing behind him badgering him about opening presents early. Pete stood by her side, adding his own farewell. It felt so natural to stand next to Jan as the guests left.

Alexis slipped out the door as well, then gave a brief hug to Jan. "Thanks for inviting me. It was nice to have some company."

"You're always welcome, Alex."

The friendship that has blossomed between the ex-military bodyguard and Jan seemed an odd pairing, but Pete wouldn't question it. Perhaps their time at the safehouse had forged a deeper connection than he would have expected.

Finally, Jo and Aiden made their way to the car with an exhausted Landon clinging to Aiden's neck.

Jo whispered goodbye. "We will see you in the morning. Maybe around 9?"

"Sounds good to me," Jan replied.

"You'll be there, Pete?" Aiden's question made Pete smile.

"Wouldn't miss it." Seeing Landon open presents on Christmas morning would be the perfect way to start the day. It was also an invitation he'd never received before. Christmas Eve dinner at Jan's house following the church service was always a crowded affair, with anyone welcome. But Christmas morning? That had always been reserved for family. And if the invitation wasn't enough, judging by Aiden's gesture during the dancing after dinner, Pete had the blessing of Jan's son to be part of the family.

Then the last car pulled away and it was just Jan and himself. "Want a cup of coffee?" Jan's invitation sounded nervous. Was she as reluctant to end the evening as he was?

"Decaf?" He knew he'd be up all night if he drank coffee this late in the evening.

Jan shrugged. "Does that make me old?"

"Probably. But if so, you're in good company. Coffee sounds great."

When Pete had finally made his way to the front door after coffee, he pressed the button on his keys to start his truck. Then he pulled on his shoes and coat before turning back to Jan. The edges of her sweater were wrapped around her small frame and she leaned against the wall.

"I wish I didn't have to go," he admitted.

"Me too," she said sadly.

He pulled her in for a kiss, but forced himself to pull back before it grew too deep. It was late and they were both tired. "I'll be back in the morning, okay?"

She nodded and he kissed her again.

"Good night, Janet."

"Good night, Petey." She emphasized the nickname and smiled mischievously.

The next morning, Pete eagerly pulled the keys

from the ignition as he arrived at Jan's house again. It was barely seven, but he knew Jan would be awake. They had the early riser gene in common.

The early morning air formed clouds of smoke as he stepped across the fresh snow to her door. A white Christmas. That was special, even in Freedom where it seemed there was an extra dose of Christmas magic each year. He knocked the snow from his boots and then rapped a knuckle on the door.

It swung open, and Jan ushered him inside. He smiled at the sight of the slippers she wore—fuzzy pink boots.

"Come on in. I haven't even put the coffee on, but you're welcome to start with a cinnamon roll." She was walking toward the kitchen, but Pete grabbed her hand and tugged her back.

"Good morning." Jan wouldn't meet his eyes. He ducked down to find hers. "I said, good morning."

Jan rolled her eyes with a smile. "I haven't even brushed my teeth yet, Pete."

He kissed her anyway. "You know if we get married, that's going to happen from time to time."

"Fine. But we're not married yet, so let me start the coffee and go brush my teeth." Her tone was firm and a bit petulant.

Pete laughed but released her. She had said 'yet'

and it was maybe his new favorite word in the English language.

While the coffee brewed, Jan disappeared upstairs, and Pete opened the Bible app on his phone. He wanted to find a Christmas Day devotional he and Jan could do together over coffee. Maybe it could be a new routine—when they were married.

JAN WET her hair and tamed the hairs that tended to get spiky overnight. Pete had seen her like this? She looked like a punk rocker. All she needed were some tattoos and a black wrist cuff.

Oh well, he had been right. If they were married, he would see her in greater disarray than this.

Still, she felt a bit harried that she was up later than usual. Last night had worn her out, but the late hour had been worth every precious memory she would treasure.

When she got back downstairs, Jan stopped short of the entrance to the kitchen. The coffee was done, and Pete was pouring himself a cup.

He turned and held up the mug. "Can I get you one?"

Everything about the moment felt right. She stepped across the kitchen and into Pete's arms. If he was surprised, he didn't show it. He set down the coffee and leaned back against the counter.

"Merry Christmas," she said. Then she pressed up and kissed him, thrilled with his eager response.

When the kiss ended, Pete looked a little shell-shocked. "Merry Christmas to you too."

Jan smiled and reached around for the mug he had poured. She settled onto one of the barstools and drank in the warm aroma of the coffee.

They sat like that, in companionable silence for a few minutes, while the sunrise lightened the sky outside the window.

"I could get used to this," Pete remarked.

"Definitely wouldn't turn down more mornings like this one." Most of her mornings were spent working early at the store, but perhaps it was time to hand off the reins to another baker.

She'd used the coffee shop as a shield for too long, so she wouldn't have to get too close to anyone or spend too much time alone. Now, she was closer to Pete than she'd ever felt before. And if she was reading Pete's intentions correctly, she wouldn't be dealing with loneliness anymore either.

Pete guided them through the Christmas devotional. It was all about acknowledging all of the blessings from God this past year, and comparing those with the ultimate gift He had given by sending His son to the world.

It couldn't have come at a more perfect time, because she was feeling extraordinarily blessed to have not only Pete, but Aiden and the rest of her family as well. The store was doing well, her health was good. But all of it paled in comparison to the gift of salvation offered due to Jesus.

"What gifts or blessings has God given you this year? How does your thankfulness for those gifts compare to your thankfulness for the gift of Jesus?" Pete read the question from the app on his phone, then paused a beat before continuing. "I have to admit the last two days I've been extremely grateful to the Lord." His smile made her blush. "But it hasn't really been about Christmas at all. I'm so glad we are at this place together now, but I have to remind myself it is still temporary. God's salvation is eternal, though."

Jan nodded. She wasn't offended by his words. In fact, the older she became, the more she had to recognize the temporal nature of this life. Once she lost a few people she loved, that eternal perspective could sometimes be the only thing that kept her going. "I think that's a great point. We have to be grateful for the blessings we are given in this life, but we also can't hold them too tightly."

Pete was watching her closely as she spoke, and Jan grew nervous under his intense gaze. Did he disagree? His eyes were warm though. "You're exactly right. I love you, Jan."

Jan flushed with pleasure as he touched her hand. This man made her heart do somersaults, yet made her feel rock solid for the first time in years. "I love you, too."

EPILOGUE

New Year's Eve was a young person's holiday, Pete decided. He loosened his tie and checked his watch. Only eleven? Couldn't they have watched the ball drop at ten so he could kiss Jan and go to sleep?

Of course, Jan was absolutely in her element, catching up with what seemed like every resident of Freedom at the party held at Freedom Ridge Resort. Her dark-green dress sparkled under the lights, and Pete thought he'd never seen her more beautiful. Perhaps it was the added knowledge that they were finally a couple after years of friendship. He no longer had to dampen the feelings of longing he'd held for too many years.

He stepped next to Jan and wrapped his arm

around her waist as he said hello to Heath and Claire.

Heath shook his hand. "Good to see you again."

"You too. Hope you got a bit of a break for the holiday."

Claire laughed. "A break? This guy?"

Heath gave a dry laugh in return. "Ha-ha. I did actually take four days off, so don't listen to her."

"Did you happen to see my message?" Pete felt Jan tense under his arm, and he rubbed her back to try to reassure her.

"I did. If you are serious about selling, Got Your Six would love to buy the safehouse. When we don't use it for clients, we can use it for staff retreats and training exercises."

What a great solution. "That's perfect. I'm glad it will work for you. I'll send over some paperwork next week and we can work out the details."

"Sounds good. Happy New Year, you two. I'm glad you've worked things out." Heath glanced at his arm around Jan's waist.

Pete only tightened his grip and smiled. He might have been a secret agent, but it was no secret he loved this woman.

When Heath and Claire stepped away, Jan turned to him. "You're selling the safe house?"

Pete nodded. "Yep. What you said about trust? I realized I had some trust issues of my own with

God's plan. Rationally, I don't need a safehouse with —as you put it—more weapons than the entire Freedom PD."

Jan dropped her face into her hands. "Did I really say that?"

"Mmm-hmmm. But that's okay. You were probably right. It was overkill. I've been out for a decade, have no reason to believe we will ever be targeted again, and I trust that God will open the doors for protection if we need them. I don't need to keep a fortress. He's my fortress."

Jan lifted her face to his and he gladly gave in to her silent request for a kiss.

After the kiss, Pete stifled a yawn. "Sorry. Long day." He'd spent the afternoon clearing old files from his office and cleaning out everything he wanted to keep from the safehouse.

"New Year's Eve is kind of a young man's holiday, isn't it?"

Pete choked on his drink. "Yes! I'm dying here."

"Come on, old man. Let's get you home."

Pete shook his head. He had plans for midnight. "No, no. We can stay."

Jan shrugged. "I really don't mind going."

"Are you sure? It's not even midnight."

"That's okay. We'll have our own countdown at the house." She wiggled her eyebrows and Pete laughed. Maybe it would be better. He would much rather kiss her with some privacy. And maybe the other thing would be better without an audience, too.

They made their way to the door, saying goodbye to a few more people as they went. Pete helped her into the truck, which was already running.

Instead of driving to her house though, Pete went to the overlook and parked. You couldn't see much of the mountains, except by the light of the moon. But the stars. On the clear, brisk night, the stars were on glorious display.

"I thought you were tired," Jan said, teasing.

Pete shrugged. "I am. But I'm also not ready to say good night to you." He opened his door. "Come on. Let's sit on the tailgate for a minute."

He helped Jan up and handed her the blanket he'd grabbed from the backseat. He didn't get up next to her though.

Instead, Pete sank to the ground on one knee and extended the ring in his hand.

Jan's eyes were wide with surprise, and her sharp intake of air was followed quickly by a warm "Oh" and a smile.

"Janet Clark, maybe it seems fast to do this so soon after we have overcome the distance between us after Thanksgiving, but I don't want to waste any time. I've known you deeply and admired you for a decade. You are my closest friend and the one my soul loves. I thought for me this day might never come—the day I finally find someone I want to spend my life with. I know it's different for you, having a wonderful life with James that was interrupted in the middle. But if you feel even a fraction of the love for me that I do for you, I know we can make a life just as beautiful. Will you marry me?"

Jan jumped off the tailgate, the blanket sliding from her shoulders. She pulled him to his feet. "It's not different for me. My life with James was beautiful in its own way. It was a different season. But I never thought the day would come when I would find someone new. And yet, there you were all along. Of course I'll marry you. I love you!"

At her declaration, Pete wrapped his arms around her waist and pulled her close, capturing her lips with his. The cold of the midnight air barely registered as he was overwhelmed with the warm sensation of their kiss. A moment later, his watch beeped, like it always did on the hour. It interrupted their kiss, and Pete chucked as he pulled away, grabbing her hand and sliding the ring on her left hand.

"Happy New Year, my love."

"Happy New Year," Jan echoed.

They kissed again, and Pete had no doubt this would be the best year yet.

Jan's Pumpkin Snickerdoodles

3 1/4 cups all-purpose flour (spooned and leveled)
3 1/2 teaspoon cornstarch
1 teaspoon cream of tartar
1 teaspoon baking soda
1/2 teaspoon baking powder
1/2 teaspoon (heaping) salt
1 1/2 teaspoon ground cinnamon
1/2 teaspoon ground ginger
1/2 teaspoon ground nutmeg
1/4 teaspoon ground allspice
1 cup granulated sugar
3/4 cup packed light brown sugar
1 cup unsalted butter, softened
1 large egg yolk
3/4 cup canned pure pumpkin puree
1 1/2 teaspoon vanilla extract

For Rolling:
1/4 cup granulated sugar
1 1/2 teaspoon ground cinnamon

Jan's Pumpkin Snickerdoodles

1. In a large mixing bowl whisk together flour, cornstarch, cream of tartar, baking soda, baking powder, salt, cinnamon, ginger, nutmeg and allspice.
2. In the bowl of an electric stand mixer fitted with the paddle attachment, cream together butter, granulated sugar and brown sugar until just combined.
3. Mix in egg yolk, then mix in pumpkin and vanilla extract.
4. With mixer set on low speed, slowly add in dry ingredients then mix until combined.
5. Cover with plastic wrap and chill 1 hour
6. Preheat oven to 350 degrees.
7. In a small bowl, whisk together 1/4 cup granulated sugar with 1 1/2 tsp cinnamon.
8. Roll dough into balls and coat in cinnamon sugar mixture.
9. Place dough balls 2-inches apart on parchment paper-lined baking sheets.
10. Bake in preheated oven 12 - 14 minutes. Cookies should look just slightly under-baked as they'll cook slightly once removed from oven. Cool on baking sheet about 5 minutes then transfer to a wire rack to cool completely.

BOOK 10 OF THE HEROES OF FREEDOM RIDGE

Curious about Tuck and Patience? Read their story in Friends with the Hero, book 10 of The Heroes of Freedom Ridge.

Can a chance encounter with a former childhood best friend be the start of a beautiful romance?

When volunteer firefighter Frank "Tuck" Tucker responds to a false alarm in the middle of the night at the new bake shop in town, he doesn't expect to come face to face with his childhood best friend. In her nightgown no less.

He also didn't expect to get hired as her new assistant. But that happened, too. Along with an odd tingling in his hand when they shook that didn't used to be there when they dug for crawfish down by the creek. But he needs a job and hers was the only place in town hiring. She didn't seem to care that his former career as a smoke jumper didn't provide much experience in baking cakes.

Patience Martel isn't sure what caused her smoke alarm to go off, but she's grateful for the malfunction. She hadn't seen Tuck since her school days, and she was thrilled to actually have someone in her shop she could trust not to steal her blind, unlike her ex. She won her court case against him, but he'd already spent the money he'd stolen and she ended up with nothing but a bunch of lawyer's fees.

Even if he's never made anything but mud pies and river stew, Tuck is a sight for sore eyes. Could he also be just what her aching heart needs, too?

Return to Freedom, Colorado and enjoy the faith, friendships, and forever-afters of the Heroes of Freedom Ridge in this Christian Christmas Romance.

Heroes of Freedom Ridge Series

(Year 1)
Rescued by the Hero (Aiden and Joanna)
Mandi Blake
Love Pact with the Hero (Jeremiah and Haven)
Liwen Y. Ho

(Year 2)
Healing the Hero (Daniel and Ashley)
Elle E. Kay
Stranded with the Hero (Carson and Nicole)
Hannah Jo Abbott

(Year 3)
Reunited with the Hero (Max and Thea)
M.E. Weyerbacher
Forgiven by the Hero (Derek and Megan)
Tara Grace Ericson

(Year 4)
Guarded by the Hero (Heath and Claire)
Mandi Blake
Trusting the Hero (Ty and Addison)
Hannah Jo Abbott

(Year 5)

Other Books in the Heroes of Freedom Ridge Series

Believing the Hero (Pete and Jan)
Tara Grace Ericson
Friends with the Hero (Tuck and Patience)
Jessie Gussman

(Year 6)
Persuaded by the Hero (Bryce and Sabrina)
Elle E. Kay
Romanced by the Hero (Mac and Amy)
Liwen Y. Ho

OTHER BOOKS BY TARA GRACE ERICSON

BOOKS BY TARA GRACE ERICSON

The Main Street Minden Series

Falling on Main Street

Winter Wishes

Spring Fever

Summer to Remember

Kissing in the Kitchen: A Main Street Minden Novella

The Bloom Sisters Series

Hoping for Hawthorne - A Bloom Family Novella

A Date for Daisy

Poppy's Proposal

Lavender and Lace

Longing for Lily

Resisting Rose

Dancing with Dandelion

Heroes of Freedom Ridge (multi-author series)

Forgiven by the Hero

Believing the Hero

ABOUT THE AUTHOR

Tara Grace Ericson lives in Missouri with her husband and three sons. She studied engineering and worked as an engineer for many years before embracing her creative side to become a full-time author. Now, she spends her days chasing her boys and writing books when she can.

She loves cooking, crocheting, and reading books by the dozen. Her writing partner is usually her black lab - Ruby - and a good cup of coffee or tea. Tara unashamedly watches Hallmark movies all winter long, even though they are predictable and cheesy. She loves a good "happily ever after" with an engaging love story. That's why Tara focuses on writing clean contemporary romance, with an emphasis on Christian faith and living. She wants to encourage her readers with stories of men and women who live out their faith in tough situations.

ACKNOWLEDGMENTS

When God called me to step out in faith and start a collaborative series, I had no idea what He would accomplish through it. So first and foremost – Father, I am so unbelievably grateful for opportunities you have given me. For this book and all the others – but especially the friends I have made while walking in (sometimes reluctant) obedience.

Those friends include the amazing Mandi Blake and Hannah Jo Abbott. Ladies, I don't know if I could have survived 2020 or 2021 without you. I thank the Lord for you every day.

This series could not have been what it is without the other authors as well – Liwen Ho, Elle E. Kay, and Jessie Gussman; thank you for jumping on board this crazy vision and making it a thousand times more than I ever expected. Thanks for being wonderful human beings to work with.

Writing Pete and Jan's story was a welcome challenge. I desperately wanted them both to get the story they deserved, but I questioned so many times my ability to write it. Extra thanks go to my beta readers, Trudy and Vicci, for helping me question my own assumptions and point out things I never would have considered! Also, thank you to Judy and Susan for proofreading the manuscript after it was finished.

Thank you to Brandi from Editing Done Write for fixing a million misplaced commas and patiently correcting me every time I insist on typing the digit instead of spelling out the number!

Lastly, thank you to my amazing husband. You are endlessly patient, accommodating, and encouraging as I pursue this crazy dream. I love doing life with you and you are, without a doubt, my favorite human.

Mister B, Little C, and Baby L… Mama loves you beyond words.

Made in the USA
Middletown, DE
12 February 2022